Three Live

Nigel Parsons

This book is dedicated to Paz, and to others like her who have the courage of their convictions to question the official narrative, rather than blindly follow the herd.

AUTHOR'S NOTE

'Three Lives' is a work of fiction. Some readers may find the views expressed by the protagonists controversial, but they are the views of fictional characters and do not reflect the author's own views.

It could be argued that, even if the opinions expressed are disagreeable to some, a cursory perusal of social media and chats at places such as bus stops show that they nonetheless exist and are held by significant numbers within society, particularly outside the bubbles of the liberal urban 'intelligentsia' and the mainstream media. To ignore this truth and dismiss such opinions out of hand as only belonging to an irrelevant extremist fringe, or to pretend that widespread opposition to the current political narrative doesn't exist, is not just delusional and self-defeating, but also a more dangerous path than acknowledging that different viewpoints do exist and engaging constructively with them.

Nigel Parsons, October 2023

PROLOGUE

A lone figure sat on a concrete bench across the river Thames from the palace of Westminster. It was an old man, thin and bony, but his one good eye was alert and full of intelligence. He was wearing a black hoodie and jogging bottoms with bright white trainers, and he shivered slightly, either from the cool early autumn weather or from excitement.

A small backpack sat next to him on the bench, and at his feet a little fluffy white dog waited patiently: some sort of mongrel but, judging by its big eyes, clearly with a bit of Cavalier King Charles in it. It was October 2034, and the sky was a mixture of sun and puffy white clouds, the latter scudding rapidly by high above while a brisk breeze ruffled the water's surface.

The timing was perfect; it was almost 200 years to the day since the palace of Westminster had been destroyed by fire, to be replaced by this gothic Elizabethan pile. He'd have preferred it to be exactly the right day for the anniversary, but this was close enough. It had been more important to wait for a day when the undersized and dysfunctional debating chamber was packed to the rafters, which was provided not by any debate about one of the great issues of the day, but by the members of parliament debating their own annual pay increase. That always got a full house. The House of Troughers, he called it.

He leaned forward in anticipation as a wisp of smoke trailed out of a lower window, then marvelled when a bright wall of flame suddenly burst into view with a huge *whoosh*, windows shattered and the smoke billowed. The flames took hold incredibly quickly, hungrily devouring ancient wooden panelling, floors and doors, fanned by the breeze. In the distance, the wail of emergency vehicles started up.

The figure chuckled and whispered a quiet 'Whoopi-de-do-da, burn, piggies, burn' to himself. He knew Bella would have loved it, and been proud of him.

He dug into the backpack to pull out a packet of popcorn and a Thermos of tea, and sat back to enjoy the spectacle, which was quite the most beautiful sight he had ever seen. The dog jumped up next to him on the bench.

'Fancy some popcorn as well, do you, Bowser?' he asked, scratching behind the dog's ears.

CHAPTER ONE

A Splendid Idea

'Christ, Edinburgh is a shitty city in a shitty country,' muttered Hugh de Sommerville, as he stood by the window. Black clouds were rolling across the city from the east, threatening yet more rain. 'I need a break. But then the trouble with travelling is that you always take yourself with you, *n'est pas?*'

He raised an eyebrow and turned to look at his roommate, but Miles wasn't listening.

Hugh was just short of six feet, twenty-three years old, with slightly awkward gangly limbs after a late growth spurt, a concave chest, and a mop of blond hair above a short back and sides. Standing up as straight as he could, he looked a bit like a back-to-front question mark.

It was 1973 and the last week of the third year of his philosophy degree at Edinburgh University; it was a four-year course, and he'd learnt next to nothing, except that philosophy could be pretty much whatever you wanted it to be. The room smelled vaguely of unwashed socks and last night's fish and chips.

Unfashionably dressed in faded yellow corduroy trousers and one of those V-neck pullovers with diamond patterns all over it, Hugh opened one of the ancient leaded windows, lit a cigarette, and tried again. 'I said...'

'I heard you,' muttered Miles, wrestling with a Scalextric controller, grimacing as he lurched this way and that like a drunken sailor. 'I'm busy.'

Hugh turned from the window, cigarette in mid-air, with a look of surprise. Despite almost two years sharing digs with Miles, he still wasn't used to being grunted at. He was more accustomed to giving orders, or at least being listened to, after an upbringing that some might have called privileged, but to him seemed just a part of the natural order of things. There were those people who simply exuded an aura of being born to rule, and Hugh felt he was one of them. *Entitled* was how he might have put it.

'Busy? You're racing toy motorbikes on a kids' game, while I have a serious point to make—'

'Fuck! I've come off! That's you, that is... okay, I'm not hurt, thanks for asking, I'm back up, I can still make a record lap, full throttle.'

'Of *course* you're not bloody hurt! It's a game, it's a toy for Christ's sake, it's—'

'It's more real than the crap that comes out of your mouth sometimes! Do you like my new layout? Took me ages to put it together.' Miles sighed as he put the controller down and the miniature bike ground to a halt.

The layout *was* quite impressive. Not just a figure of eight, it also boasted a pit stop, tiny flag-waving figures for crowds, a chicane, a little man with a chequered flag, and a tunnel topped with a church.

Miles ran a hand through his thick, wiry black hair. Physically, he was the opposite of his friend: at least three inches shorter, swarthy, with a taut, wiry build and square chin covered in dark stubble. He spoke with a Cornish rhoticity that reflected his tin miner and fishermen forebears. The difference was also sartorial, with Miles sporting nearly worn-out flared jeans and a tie-dyed T-shirt along with his long unruly locks. But they had formed an unlikely companionship, forged as much as anything by the general animosity both had endured from the beginning of their time in the Scottish capital: Hugh because of his unmistakeable upper-class Englishness, Miles because he was from about as far south of Scotland as it was possible to get in the United Kingdom, which, among the nationalist bigots, was enough to make him a confirmed southern Sassenach despite his Celtic roots.

'What were you going on about again?' Miles asked.

'I was saying that the trouble with travel is that you always take yourself with you. Well, that and I need a break from this place.' Hugh blew a cloud of blue smoke out of the window. 'I mean if you're an arsehole and go to Bali or the Atacama Desert or somewhere, you'll still be an arsehole when you get there, and still be one when you get back.'

'Is that the kind of rubbish they teach you in philosophy?'

'What do you mean, rubbish?'

'Well, of course you bloody well take yourself with you. What else are you going to do, leave yourself behind? Have an out-of-body experience?'

Hugh flicked his butt out into the courtyard below and shut the window again to keep out the permanently cold air. 'No, I meant the inner you, obviously not the physical you. You know, they say 'get away from it all', but you don't, do you? Because no matter where you go, you are still you, with all the same hang-ups, problems, likes and dislikes.'

Miles picked up his controller again to select a new speed. 'Bollocks. You need to get out a bit more, mate. Now I need to focus, so...'

'Maybe you're right; maybe an out-of-body experience is the answer. You know, that's actually a splendid idea!'

'Let me know when you're back in this world; we'll go for a pint.'

'Whatever. I'm going for a walk.' Hugh pulled on his overcoat and headed for the door, throwing a bright red scarf around his neck just as a vicious gust of wind hurled a spray of rain against the window, as if someone had thrown a handful of pebbles against the glass. The day, if you could call it that, had suddenly noticeably darkened.

'Good fucking luck with that, then,' muttered Miles, sending his small yellow motorbike straight at the start line and settling deeper into his stained fake leopard skin beanbag. He clamped a set of headphones on and leaned over to drop the nearby turntable's needle onto his beloved Black Sabbath LP.

He vaguely heard the door shut and didn't realise until hours later, when he woke up on the beanbag with his headphones still in place and the record player needle bumping uselessly around the centre of the LP, that the honourable Hugh hadn't returned.

CHAPTER TWO

The Magical Ship

Jennings cursed as his glass eye fell out again and dropped into his partially consumed porridge. The eye was too small. A new one was being made but, in the meantime, it was either stick with the ill-fitting model, or wear a patch and put up with the endless braindead pirate 'jokes' that that inevitably invoked.

'Aye aye,' said Spencer from the other side of the table, to barely concealed mirth from those around.

Jennings glared at him with his one good eye while he fished around in the porridge for its glass companion, found it and licked off the excess lumps of oats before rinsing it in his glass of Ribena.

'Ew,' muttered someone further down.

'You think it's funny to only have one eye, do you? I can still have your guts for garters, you – you fat carrot-top berk,' Jennings hissed at Spencer. While big, Spencer was not exactly fat, but he was a coward. And he had a shock of bright orange hair.

'Aye… er, no, I just meant—'

A spoonful of porridge hit Spencer square in the face, followed by the spoon itself, and pandemonium briefly broke out before the table prefect slammed his fist down to demand silence.

'Right, you two, Mr Green's study – now!'

Jennings and Spencer rose from their respective benches and slunk off to the housemaster's study, Spencer wiping the sticky grey gruel from his cheeks with a grubby handkerchief.

They knew what awaited them; Mr Green had infamously stuck a nail through the top of his desk so that half an inch protruded underneath, where those due a beating had to put their heads. If they flinched, they got the nail in the head as well as the stick on their backsides.

'Bollocks to this,' muttered Jennings as he slouched behind Spencer, sweeping up an old newspaper from a sideboard and stuffing it down the back of his trousers. He had blond, almost white hair, with one pale grey red-rimmed eye, which only added to his albino look despite the mismatched brown glass eye. Although slightly built – some might say scrawny – he was scrawny in a street fighting kind of way. From his face to his elbows to his ankles he was all bony angles, and he exuded a barely stifled aggression that made most steer clear of him. He hated the school, a Victorian pile buried in the English countryside; he was always cold, always hungry, and mostly angry.

And life had started so well, he mused as he sat outside the housemaster's study, watching dust motes dance in the pale winter sunshine filtering through grubby sash windows.

When Jennings looked back, the first eight years had been like a fairy tale. That is, apart from losing his right eye when trying to pry some string from a chair leg with a pair of scissors; that was when he learnt that you should always cut away from yourself, not towards, and certainly not towards your face.

Eight perfect years, and then life had suddenly and inexplicably come to a halt. That was seven years ago, in 1959. Seven years of unmitigated misery, of sleeping on cast-iron beds with a thin mattress and a threadbare blanket to keep out the cold – which it didn't. Seven years of pointless running along country lanes in pouring rain, of beatings both taken and given, of forcing down food you wouldn't give to your dog, of playing soldiers in the Brecon Beacons and using that nonce May to wank him off whenever he needed it. Well, the wanking was tolerable; it would be a couple more years yet before he tasted the delights of that forbidden fruit, a woman, and, in the meantime, beggars couldn't be choosers.

He leaned back and dozed against a radiator, remembering his once-warm home, struggling to his first school through the Aberdeen snow with an oversized satchel on his back. Afterwards he would watch *Rag, Tag and Bobtail* on their tiny black-and-white box television as he tucked into Spam fritters, or whatever was available that day; the rationing had ended a couple of years earlier, but food still wasn't plentiful. Then it was London for a few months, which he didn't remember much about, only getting his ears boxed until he lost his Scottish accent and learnt to speak like a Londoner, and his father swapping his improbable kilt for an even more improbable suit and bowler hat as befitted the War Office. And then it was onto the ship, that *magical* ship.

Her Majesty's Troopship *Devonshire*, it was called. A bit of a rust bucket, in truth; an old German ship refitted and renamed for carrying the families of members of the British armed services across the globe, to populate the innumerable garrisons that represented the greatest empire the world had ever known, and to live a life they could only dream about back home.

Military bands marched up and down the Liverpool docks and hundreds of women and children waved Union Jacks under gunmetal skies, giving them a rousing send-off, as the ship's lines were cast off and two tugboats pulled them slowly towards the open sea.

Because Jennings' father was a major, they were on one of the higher decks with two adjoining cabins, both with portholes: one for Jennings and his ghastly older sister Daphne (who in their right mind called their daughter Daphne?), with whom he bickered constantly, and one for the adults. A couple of decks below were the ORs, the Other Ranks, the squaddies, most of them young and single, virgin soldiers on their way to fight the uprising in Malaya. But they didn't mix much with the officer class.

They called it the officer class, but really, thanks to the war, their ranks had been filled by a variety of lower orders. Jennings' own father, the son of a milkman, had eagerly joined up and lost everything – his home, his two brothers, his parents, his aunt Maude – when a V2 had scored a direct hit on their house in Wood Green. With nothing to go back to, the army had become his family and he'd risen through the ranks.

Jennings vividly remembered the day when the chill Atlantic air had been replaced by the warmth of the Mediterranean, then later the heat of the Suez Canal, and their winter clothes were stowed away for good. In the Suez, he and the other children amused themselves by throwing farthings and halfpennies into the water and watching the natives waiting in wooden canoes below dive in after them, secretly hoping for the water to explode into a bloody froth as a shark attacked, but it never happened. In Aden there was a goat that ate cigarettes for a small fee, and in Colombo crashing waves in a warm sea.

The Indian Ocean was vast. For days they saw no land or birds as the children sat learning nothing at rows of desks on the upper deck, instead watching the dolphins and flying fish in the glistening sea, while the menfolk shot balloons out of the sky and the women talked over endless cups of tea.

They celebrated crossing the equator with all manner of japes, first-timers getting the rough end of Neptune's commandments, followed by a glittering ball in the evening, all the grown-ups dressed in extravagant gowns and tails. At last they passed through the Malacca Strait to reach Singapore, where another marching band waited to greet them almost five whole weeks after the last one had bidden them farewell.

Mr Green's door was flung open and the man himself stood glaring at the two miscreants, who had jumped up from their reveries.

'You first, Jennings!' he commanded.

CHAPTER THREE

THE CURIOSITY SHOP

Fiona Gordon, 'Fi' to her friends, walked slowly along Edinburgh's Royal Mile until she found the small alleyway that housed her tiny book and curiosity shop.

Small, with greying hair under her black hood, she presented more than a passing resemblance to a penguin, with her slightly hunched shoulders, small quick steps and myopic gaze permanently fixed on the ground in front of her. This resemblance became even more marked if she was happy, when she was in the habit of flapping her arms up and down, as though trying to fly. But today it was drizzling and the wind from the North Sea was biting, too strong to unfurl the umbrella, so there was no flapping of arms.

As she stopped to fumble for the door keys buried in her voluminous multicoloured bag, she suddenly realised there was a body slumped in the doorway, partially covered by a sodden cardboard box and with a bright red scarf around its neck. Fiona hesitated, then gingerly reached out with her umbrella and poked the prostrate figure gently with the tip.

'Excuse me,' she said, poking harder.

She jumped back in alarm as the body suddenly lurched into life, throwing off its cardboard covering. A young man with a mop of blond hair and a nose the colour of an overripe strawberry stared up at her, blinking in confusion.

'So sorry, but you're blocking my doorway – are you all right?' Fiona leaned forwards again, trying to bring the young face into focus.

'Ma'am, the apologies are all mine!' Hugh stammered (for it was he, of course). 'I didn't mean to frighten you.' He slowly unwound and pushed himself to his feet, groaning at his stiff joints and stretching skywards. 'On the contrary, ma'am, I was waiting for the shop to open. I saw the notice in your window, and it seemed like a message, it—'

'What are you blathering on about, young man? What notice? Why couldn't you come back at a proper time? Ach, well, you'd better come in and have something hot to drink; you look like shite and ye'll catch yer death oot here.'

Fiona found her key and unlocked the door, pushing it open over a pile of flyers and bills, which she kicked to one side as the bell tinkled a welcome. 'Right, sit yersel' there, then,' she said, indicating a worn wingback chair and giving Hugh an equally worn tartan rug. 'What'll it be? Cup of tea, milk and sugar?'

Hugh sank gratefully into the chair, draping the rug around his shoulders, and nodded. 'Two sugars, please.' His teeth were chattering, but his nose was slowly returning to its normal colour.

'You're a Sass then, are you?' Fiona asked. 'What are you doing this far north?'

'A what? Oh, right, a Sassenach; yes, I'm English. I'm at the university—'

'So, what's all this nonsense about a notice? What is it yer after?'

Hugh blinked a couple of times and tried to explain. 'Er, well, it's the one about out-of-body experiences, you see—'

'Out-of-body experiences, you say? Well, that's a new one, even with all the weirdos about these days. Some sort of hippy rubbish, is it?'

After leaving Miles, Hugh had trod the glistening cobbles of Edinburgh in a funk, his mind whirring; he took life far too seriously. Eventually he'd ducked into a gloomy pub and ordered a pint of heavy, then another, and another, until his world began to spin.

When the pub had shut, he'd wandered aimlessly until he had come to the small curiosity shop and spotted the sign, which in his inebriated state seemed like a sign from heaven. He'd meant to return to his rooms but decided on a quick nap first, making himself comfortable in the doorway with the help of a large cardboard box, which was where Fiona had found him still snoring early the next morning.

'No, I'm not a hippy – short hair, you see? No flowers in there. But, well, I'm studying philosophy and, er, and I was having this conversation about how we always take ourselves with us when we travel, and—'

'Philosophy? Load of ruddy nonsense if you ask me; just common sense wrapped up in fancy jargon,' Fiona turned on a Primus stove to boil the water and busied herself with cups. Hugh watched as she warmed a small white porcelain teapot, then put three spoons of loose tea inside, one for each cup and one for the pot. 'An out-of-body experience, you say? More ruddy nonsense if you ask me, not that ye were asking, mind. Here, this'll warm you up. Can't find my tea strainer, mind, so there'll be a few leaves inside, but they'll soon sink to the bottom.'

'There's a sign in your window,' Hugh explained as he gratefully accepted the proffered cup of tea and wrapped his hands around it to warm them up.

'Is there, now?' Fiona went to the window and peered at the various signs there. 'Ah, this'll be the one,' she said, picking at the Sellotape and peeling off a yellowing piece of paper. 'Will ye look at that, now? Forgotten it was there. *Do you want an out-of-body experience?*' she read out loud. '*Join us in the depths of the Amazon forest for the ultimate ayahuasca trip.*' Well, I don't know about that, it's no me offering it, but there's a number here – are ye sure about this? Sounds a bit daft if you ask me...'

Hugh took the paper from her. 'Leticia,' he said. 'Where's that?'

'How would I know? They just pay me to advertise their rubbish.'

Hugh took a notebook from his pocket, wrote down the number and studied the paper. 'Colombia,' he said. 'It's in Colombia.' His face had taken on a dreamy look. 'It really is like a message.'

'Like in Canada, you mean?'

'No, no, not British Columbia; Colombia, the South American

country. It's a London number... can I use your phone? I'll pay you.'

'I suppose. It's long-distance, mind; won't be cheap. It'll be a florin at least.' Fiona looked dubious.

Hugh dug in his pocket and fished out two shillings.

'Aye, that should do it. Don't be long, mind.' She indicated an avocado-coloured telephone sitting on a pile of books.

'Can I use the bathroom first?'

CHAPTER FOUR

Singapore

'Now then, Jennings, what is it this time?' Mr Green asked wearily as he shut the door behind them.

In his early fifties, with watery pale blue eyes and thinning faded brown hair combed over his scalp, the housemaster was dressed in the customary black gown that all the teachers wore. His trousers were unpressed, his shoes dull brown lace-ups, and his sleeveless pale grey pullover betrayed a couple of spots from his morning's boiled eggs. In his hand he held a thin cane, but, despite his stern countenance, he actually had a soft spot for young Jennings.

'It's my eye,' Jennings muttered miserably. 'Spencer was teasing me again. I know I shouldn't have thrown porridge at him, but he's always doing it, it's not fair...'

'Not fair, not fair; ah, if only life was fair, laddie. Well, you know the rules; three of the best this time. Bend over, head under the table.'

Jennings did as he was told. He tensed as he heard the cane swish, and then almost bumped the nail in surprise when there was no pain, not even any contact. He peered round to see Mr Green beat his armchair twice more, the dust rising in a cloud.

'Stand up, boy – our little secret this time,' Mr Green touched his nose. 'Do try to behave in future, though.'

'Yes, sir, of course, sir, thank you, sir. I—'

'Off you go now; not a word to anyone. Anyway, I can see you've stuffed newspaper down the back of your trousers. You're confined to the library until the morning break.' He smiled faintly and opened the door to let Jennings out. 'Spencer, you're next!'

As Jennings walked away, he had the satisfaction of hearing the cane come crashing down again, this time accompanied by a yelp of pain from the hapless Spencer. He chuckled and made his way to the library.

It was a large octagonal room with a musty smell, desks and benches for study, and the occasional easy chair for reading. Jennings selected a quiet corner with a comfortable-looking chair, pulled a book from the shelves so he could pretend to read, and settled down. The library was one of his favourite rooms, and even better when he'd been banished there as a punishment and had it almost to himself; it was more like a reward.

Spencer shuffled in shortly afterwards, stuck his tongue out at Jennings, and took a seat as far away from his adversary as possible.

'Carrot top,' muttered Jennings. He turned to the window to resume his daydreaming.

Singapore and Malaya had lasted just three far-too-short years. He remembered idyllic days at the Singapore Swimming Club (whites only, apart from the waiters), their huge colonial house with snakes at the bottom of the garden and the screeching monkeys just beyond, destroying columns of ants with paraffin, squatting with local kids in the street outside as they played marbles, joyous days at the army-run school, boat trips to nearby islands where they discovered the shells of giant king crabs and snorkelled among multicoloured tropical fish, and the gruesome statues at the Tiger Balm Gardens with its Ten Courts of Hell.

Occasionally they'd venture over the Causeway to Malaya to enjoy the cool of the hill station in the Cameron Highlands. Driving through Malaya in an armoured car during the uprising was exhilarating: the 'white' zones, which were considered safe, and the 'black' zones, where communist guerrillas were known to operate and it was forbidden to drive at less than sixty miles per hour. There were occasional riots in Singapore too, mostly of the brick-throwing type, so his father always wore a loaded pistol at his waist, which was pretty cool. It was very heavy, and Jennings thought it was a Browning.

There were magnificent garden parties too, the men in uniform with Sam Browne belts and leather cross straps and medal ribbons, and the women in floral summer dresses. Local servants wandered around with trays of cocktails, helped by Daphne and little Albert (for that was Jennings' first name) with plates of canapés, and everyone was smoking: the men mostly cigars, and the women cigarettes in long slender holders.

Jennings smiled as he recalled the time a brigadier, a tall and severe-looking man with a handlebar moustache, suddenly tapped him on the shoulder and asked for an egg mayonnaise. Jennings had turned so abruptly that gravity had taken over, which meant that although the plate turned with him, the food ended up on the lawn.

'Never mind, young fellow, never mind, we'll soon get that cleared up.'

'Yes, sir.' Tears were forming in his good eye.

'Now, now, nothing to get so upset about. Stiff upper lip, chest out, stomach in; that's what won the empire, boy, and the sun will never set on the British empire, hmm?'

'Yes, sir – I mean no, sir.'

In fact, the sun was already getting low in the sky as far as the empire was concerned. This was something the old warhorse had some inkling about, given that India was already gone and was wallowing in inter-religious bloodshed after Gandhi had kicked the white man out. Pakistan and Bangladesh too, but they were part of the Indian settlement. Others had joined them – Burma, Ceylon, Jordan, Libya and Palestine (Israel), and much earlier Egypt and Iraq – but young Albert had not the faintest clue about all of that. That night, though, he made a list of all the British colonies in the world and stuck it on his bedroom wall, and put a line through the ones that already left the club.

The family also had a pye-dog called Ben who was exiled to a tea plantation in Malaya after biting the postman, but who miraculously found his way back across the Causeway to their house three days later. That was a smart dog, thought Jennings, the best ever.

Those three years passed in a flash, far too quickly, and then it was back onto another ship, the nearly new HMT *Oxfordshire* this time, to make the return journey. There was again a farewell band on the quayside, this time playing 'Auld Lang Syne'.

Winter clothes in the form of hand-knitted pullovers reappeared after a brief stop at Gibraltar, and then it was into the Atlantic Ocean with its increasingly cold winds and overcast skies, all the way back to Liverpool. The place looked drab, cold and grey after the lush of the tropics, and it was. His treasured list of colonies also had several more crossings out: Malawi, South Yemen and Swaziland had also gained independence.

In the distance a bell sounded to announce the morning break, a glass of milk and biscuits, and Jennings roused himself from his stupor to obey the summons. Spencer waited until he was well out of the way before following in his footsteps.

CHAPTER FIVE

A Missing Person

Two days after Hugh's disappearance, Miles was brushing his teeth when he heard a repeated hammering at his door. He eventually opened it to be confronted by a tall, thin young policeman with his helmet under his arm.

'Can I help you?' Miles asked.

'Constable Constable, sir.'

'Sorry?'

'My name is Constable, and I'm a police constable. So it's Constable Constable.'

'That's unfortunate,' Miles replied. 'You know, my dad knew a bloke in the army called Major. So when he made sergeant major he was Sergeant Major Major. And I guess if he made major he would have been Major Major, and then maybe Colonel Major. Quite confusing…' He wondered why he was saying all these inane things, but policemen always made him feel uncomfortable and nervous, even guilty, though of course he'd done nothing wrong.

The young policeman regarded Miles, wondering if he was taking the piss, which was not uncommon. 'Be that as it may, sir, you reported a missing person?'

'Ah, yes, of course – my roommate, Hugh de Sommerville. He went out a couple of days ago, in the evening, and he never came back. He's never done anything like that before.'

'Had you had an argument, maybe?'

'No, nothing like that. He just went out and didn't come back.'

'Did he drive? Does he have a car?'

'Yes, he does, as it happens. I looked but couldn't see it in the college car park.'

'What kind of car exactly, sir?'

'It's a green one.'

Constable Constable made a note. 'Could you perhaps be more specific? Make and model, perhaps? Licence plate, maybe?'

'Oh, well, not really, I don't know much about cars; not at all interested in them, even if I could afford one. I'm more into motorbikes. But I think it was an English one.'

'Austin, maybe? Morris? Rover? Triumph?'

'Yes, that's it! A Triumph, I think. I remember because I've always wanted a Bonneville – best bikes in the world, if you ask me – but I don't know what model the car is.'

Constable Constable was losing patience. He put away his notebook. 'Well, sir, as said "missing person" is an adult he's not really missing at all, if you get my drift. People disappear all of the time; it's more common than you think. But we'll keep an eye out if you give me a description.'

Miles described Hugh to the best of his ability, then added, 'His family live in Lincolnshire, I think. I don't have the exact address – not even a telephone number, I'm afraid – but would that help?'

Constable Constable thought not, but didn't say so as he bade Miles farewell. *Fucking students,* he thought as he walked away. *Pain in the arse. Is this what I joined the force for?*

*

The car was in fact a Triumph Herald convertible, Hugh's pride and joy, which he had driven at speed down to his father's farm twenty miles outside Lincoln immediately after he'd hung up the phone at the curiosity shop.

After he had given his mother, Gladys, a perfunctory peck on the cheek in the sunroom, where she was having her customary afternoon gin and tonic, he went in search of his father, who was predictably in his study.

An older carbon copy of Hugh, Dominic de Sommerville rose from behind his desk to shake his son and heir by the hand. 'My dear boy, to what do we owe the pleasure? Surely you're not due for another week at least?'

'Can't stop, Father,' Hugh told him breathlessly. 'I'm on my way to London, got an urgent research project to undertake.' He paused, chin in hand. There was no easy way to say this. 'Thing is, I'm a bit short – you couldn't advance me a bit of my allowance, could you?'

Dominic made a sort of harrumphing sound. 'Should have guessed. What sort of advance?'

'Er, well, say three hundred pounds?'

'Three hundred pounds!' his father exclaimed. 'That's not an advance; a king's ransom, more like! Not sure I even have that much in the safe; harvest was a bit below par this year, you know, and there's been all sort of expenses. What on earth do you need that kind of money for?'

Christ, thought Hugh. *It's like getting blood out of a stone.* But what he said was, 'I'll explain later; it's a bit complicated, but it's important, I probably won't need all of it anyway, so I'll give back the extra when I see you at Christmas. Please, Father!'

Dominic harrumphed several times more, but he unlocked his safe anyway and rummaged around inside before handing a wad of bank notes to his son. 'Should be a couple of hundred or more there; it's all I can manage, I'm afraid. Will that do?'

'Brilliant! Far out! You're a brick, Father, an absolute brick. Thanks a million, and I'll see you at Christmas!' Hugh was already moving towards the door to give his mother another peck, to say goodbye this time, and shortly afterwards they heard his car spinning gravel on the driveway.

Far out? A brick? thought his father as the sound of the engine faded. *What the devil did he mean by that? Youth of today, can barely understand them.*

CHAPTER SIX

INCARCERATION

Returning from Singapore, the Jennings family were sent first to a camp in Dorset for several months, and thence to Germany to join the British Army of the Rhine.

No sooner had they arrived than young Albert Jennings, just eight years old by this time, noticed a distinctly icy atmosphere descending on the house. His mother and father engaged in furious whispered arguments in the kitchen, in the garden, in their bedroom, wherever they happened to be. His mother was often in tears, his father red-faced and distant.

It wasn't long before he discovered they were fighting over his fate. Despite fierce opposition from his mother, his father had decided he was to be sentenced to boarding school back in England. His mother, a gentle woman from the Home Counties, was loath to let him go; she wanted her children with her in the home, couldn't see the point of having children if you were just going to send them away. But a woman's opinion counted for little, and his father was adamant. Boarding school would provide 'backbone' and 'independence' (the latter being precisely what his mother didn't want him to have at such a tender age), and so he was condemned to years of misery.

The first place, a 'preparatory school', wasn't so bad, more like a country manor house with only a few dozen pupils, but he still hated it from day one and ran away within weeks. The attempted escape was futile, a single night in a hedgerow with nothing but a bar of chocolate and a fizzy drink being enough to coax him back to his prison.

Nevertheless, he threw such a fit when he went home for the

Christmas holidays that his mother finally put her foot down and point-blank refused to send him back. The best she got was a temporary reprieve for two years, but that was better than nothing. Jennings was able to slip back into the easy life of the local army school, with children of his own kind and home cooking every night. He would listen to plays on the radio with his mother and sister, with the lights turned down and a well-stocked trolley of cocktail sausages, biscuits and tea on hand.

At the weekends he enjoyed long walks in the woods with their new dog, a beautiful brown-nosed Hungarian vizsla called Czilla, and the chance to spend his pocket money on bags of lemon sherbets or gobstoppers and his weekly comics. His favourites were the war comics where a brave Tommy would inevitably jump out of a trench with his Sten gun and shout, 'Not so fast, Fritz!' or a Japanese would scream 'Aieeeee!' as he was cut down by a hail of nine-millimetre bullets. Those and the *Eagle*, with the mysterious green Mekon threatening to annihilate all Earthmen.

In the afternoons, while his mother sipped her first weak Scotch and ginger and Daphne had to do her forced piano practice, he arrayed his own armies of plastic soldiers across the floor – the British in khaki, the Germans grey, the Japanese dark green and the Russians red – and the house resounded to the sound of Albert machine-gunning down all his enemies: 'Eh-eh-eh-eh-eh, yeah, gotcha, all dead,' while his artillery fired matchsticks which soon littered the carpet. The war raged on until his father returned from golf and ordered him to clear everything up.

Occasionally he asked his father what he'd done in the war, but the answer was always the same: 'Maybe when you're older.' Albert knew his father had been a Desert Rat because he wore the tie and went to the reunions, but other than that he never spoke about it. Nor did any of the other adults. Whatever had happened to him out there in the deserts of Egypt and Tunisia was destined to stay with him until the grave.

During Albert's reprieve from boarding school his father had become ever more distant, even cold, as though he was nursing some disappointment or shame. In a way, he was.

Over everything hung the ticking of the Doomsday Clock. It was like the reverse of a prison sentence. Instead of chalking off the days to freedom, they were all counting the days until, amid more bitter tears of recrimination from Albert and his mother, he would be put back on the boat to be met by an elderly friend of the family in a flat cap and reincarcerated in the depths of the Somerset Levels.

On his last day at the army school, he held hands through the fence that divided the boys' and girls' playgrounds with Enid, the young blonde girl who had become his best friend. It was the last meaningful relationship he was to have with either a girl or a woman for at least a decade.

It wasn't long before he accepted his lot. The preparatory school was a benign enough place, and in time home life faded into the distance. But nothing had prepared him for the horrors that awaited him at the secondary school he found himself shipped off to after scraping through his Common Entrance examinations at the age of thirteen. Academically gifted he was not.

Hidden in the middle of the windswept Suffolk countryside, the school was a throwback to Victorian times, all red brick buildings with windows that didn't fit and radiators that didn't work and harsh discipline. The teachers were spectral in their long black gowns, and most still seemed to be suffering from shellshock from the war; a banged desk lid was enough to send them ducking for cover.

As the teachers walked up and down the aisles of desks, the pupils turned and flicked their ink pens onto the backs of their gowns. Matron, an ugly old hag with a hairy chin, complained constantly about all the 'coffee stains' on the boys' bedsheets, and everyone lusted after Nurse Marion, the only half-decent-looking woman for miles.

Like everyone else, Jennings spent two years as a 'fag', whose job was to act as a virtual slave for some sadistic sixth-former: clean his shoes, make his bed, dust his study, make him tea or coffee whenever he wanted, all the while risking a beating. Sixth-formers were allowed to cane those below them, who they also frequently regarded as sex objects.

Chapel had to be attended every day, unless you were one of the few Catholics; they were given homework to do instead. There were no black kids and just one Asian called Mehta, but he must have been an Anglican because he went to chapel, and he was accepted because he was fast and a good wing three-quarter back.

One day a week was devoted to the Combined Cadet Force and everyone, without exception, learnt to march, present arms, salute and play war games. Two weeks of the summer holidays were also stolen so those war games could be played in earnest in the sodden Brecon Beacons, complete with Bren guns, thunder flashes and .22 rifles loaded with blanks.

He was also always hungry; unlike other boys who lived either locally or no further than London, he never got visits from his parents to replenish his tuck box, which was always empty. The two pounds a term that his parsimonious father gave him for spending in the tuck shop never lasted more than a few weeks, especially after buying an occasional furtive packet of ten Woodbines from the nearby newsagent.

Returning to Germany for the school holidays didn't help. Most of his old friends had moved on to other postings, and there wasn't even a television to watch. He did manage a brief fling once with a neighbouring girl, and even got as far as a 'top half only' feel around, but by the following holidays she had gone as well and he was alone again with just Daphne for company. Three years his senior, Daphne was growing up fast, sprouting breasts and showing an unhealthy interest in the local German boys, and she didn't want Albert poking his nose in and spoiling her act.

Whenever the next term started, everyone else would be talking about what they'd watched on television, conversations that Jennings was excluded from, and no one was interested in hearing about his trips to Winterberg or to the Rhine or wherever he'd been dragged off to.

But the years drifted by regardless, and he survived. He would finally leave in 1968 with a couple of A-levels, not good enough for a decent university even if he'd wanted to go. He had hung on to his tattered list of British colonies, which had become something of a talisman for him, but it now contained more black lines than loyal subjects. Barbados was gone, as were Botswana, Cyprus, Gambia, Ghana, Guyana, Jamaica, Kenya, Kuwait, Lesotho, Malawi, Malaya, the Maldives, Malta, Mauritius, Nauru, Nigeria, Sierra Leone, Somaliland, South Yemen, Singapore, Sudan, Tanganyika, Trinidad and Tobago, Uganda, Zambia and Zanzibar. The brigadier's sun was almost sitting on the horizon, and the red of empire covered less and less of the globe.

He was sick of education, and instead found work on a construction site, playing his part in building horrendous concrete blocks of flats which none of the architects would dream of living in, and which paid well enough. In this way he inadvertently became part of the majority non-graduate working class, who would later become the most despised group for the ruling graduate elite, opening up huge divides in the country, economically but more importantly culturally. But that was all in the future.

The same year he left school, he saw a new X-rated film called *If*, starring Malcolm McDowell. It could almost have been filmed at his school, and it culminated in bloody insurrection. For the first time Albert, as he was again after leaving school, started to think that violence was the only answer to the stultifying world he inhabited. He was still angry.

He discovered that the outside world had moved on apace, with the Beatles, the Rolling Stones, the Kinks, Jimi Hendrix, Uriah Heep, Tyrannosaurus Rex, Bob Dylan, Leonard Cohen and countless others revolutionising the music scene, while the mods and rockers fought pitched battles and finally the hippies took over.

Albert despised the hippies almost from the get-go. He thought their clothes looked silly, the bell-bottom jeans and flowery shirts, and their dirty hair. He thought their slogans of 'make love, not war' might have meant well, but that they were naive, although he kept his thoughts to himself. His father had been right about him learning 'independence'; he'd become a loner, and that didn't change with his new freedom.

CHAPTER SEVEN

INTO THE JUNGLE

After a frantic four-hour drive through relentless rain, Hugh finally found himself in a dingy travel office in a side street off Warwick Road in London's Earl's Court. The area was known then as 'Kangaroo Valley' because of the thousands of transient Australians and New Zealanders, backpackers carrying their worldly goods on their backs like a colony of snails, who'd set up shop there, until they were replaced by the Arabs and later the Pakistanis. He had just under four hundred pounds in his pocket.

A girl with straggly blue hair and a ring through her dripping nose shuffled through a Rolodex, finally pulling a card out. 'Yeah, this is the one, man. Leytica, innit?'

'Leticia,' Hugh corrected her. 'It's in Colombia – I thought you were Latin American travel specialists?'

'Yeah, right, but there are lots of other places there, man.'

'My name is Hugh, Hugh de Sommerville.'

'Yeah, whatever, man. Says here you got to fly to Bogotá first, then catch another plane to this Leticia place. Three hundred and twenty-five all in, and that includes the ayahuasca thing. There and back in less than a week – all right? And you're in luck; the next trip leaves the day after tomorrow. It's only once a month, you know.'

'I'll take it,' said Hugh, counting out his precious notes and handing them over.

*

After two nights in a dingy bed-and-breakfast with flowered wallpaper, a sink in his room and a shared bathroom, Hugh found himself sitting in the rear smoking section of a British Caledonian flight direct to Bogotá. He'd spent the previous day maxing out his credit card on a pair of sturdy walking boots, a safari suit with pockets everywhere, and a money belt where he could hide his remaining cash. He'd also sent a brief postcard to Miles apologising for his absence, saying he'd had to rush but would explain all after the Christmas break.

Twelve hours after taking off from London's Heathrow, the aeroplane banked steeply and almost nosedived into El Dorado Airport, wedged between Andean peaks. Bogotá, sitting several thousand yards above sea level, was cold, and Hugh shivered in his totally inappropriate safari suit. Within three hours, though, after clearing immigration and miraculously being greeted by a local travel representative, he was on a second aeroplane, an Avianca wooden-hulled affair with twin propellers which did little to inspire confidence.

A little over two hours later they taxied along the runway at Leticia in the southeast of the country, and stopped outside a dilapidated building with a corrugated iron roof which constituted the arrivals hall. It was pouring with rain and oppressively hot, and suddenly the safari suit seemed like money well spent.

A couple of soldiers in green fatigues, rifles slung across their shoulders, emptied his bag and searched meticulously through his belongings, paying particular attention to his toiletries and leafing through the couple of novels he'd brought with him.

'Marijuana?' one of them asked him.

'That'd be coal to Newcastle, mate,' Hugh replied cheerfully. It was early days, but the marijuana trade was just taking off, and apparently Leticia was a major smuggling centre, lying as it did on the borders of Brazil and Peru with waterways running in all directions.

The two soldiers looked at him, debating whether a body search was more trouble than it was worth. 'Coal?' said the first.

'Just a joke, sorry.' Hugh gave his most engaging smile. 'I'm just on holiday. Tourist?'

He was waved through contemptuously to discover that, once again and astonishingly, a small man in a straw hat was waiting with a card on which was scrawled *Mr Summer*. The man looked like he might be an Indian – he had slightly Asiatic features in a brown face and twinkling eyes – but that was hardly surprising given than many of Leticia's inhabitants were still indigenous, even if the population had been swelled by several thousand poorer city folk who'd been shipped in by a Colombian government wary of Peruvian claims to the area.

Hugh made his way over and pointed at himself. 'Hugh de Sommerville.'

Three other foreigners were standing with the apparent guide, two Americans and a Canadian. One had a long ponytail, all three were bearded, and all three carried backpacks.

'You also gringo?' The guide smiled to show a mouth with half its teeth missing.

'I'm English,' Hugh said.

'Ah, Ingles, Ingles, welcome to Leticia. Not many Ingles here. Come, follow me.'

The rain had stopped, but the humidity was stultifying and the mosquitos ferocious. The damp, putrid smell of decaying tropical vegetation was overpowering. After a short bone-shaking ride in an old Willys Jeep, they stopped outside a general store in the centre of town.

Their guide, Ricaurte, jumped down. 'Come, tonight we stay here in Leticia. Tomorrow, we take the river. Follow me.'

They passed through a small square overlooked by the town hall, a red and white brick affair with the Colombian yellow, blue and red flag wilting in the heat. The square was surrounded by trees, their trunks painted white against the all-pervasive mosquitos.

Once they left the centre, the tarmac ended and they wandered down dusty side streets with a mixture of red brick houses with cement floors, lean-tos and hastily thrown up shacks, where swollen-bellied children and pregnant women stopped haranguing each other to watch their progress. After fifteen minutes or so,

Ricaurte stopped outside an ancient two-storey wooden building with steps leading up to the front porch, where a sign proudly announced *The Jungle Lodge*.

That evening Hugh joined the three others in his group at a local restaurant. He ordered some spit-roasted chicken with spicy aji sauce, while his companions opted for tamales, a mixture of rice, vegetables and shredded pork wrapped in banana leaves. Hugh also differed by ordering a black Porter-style Club Colombia beer, served cold, instead of the cheaper Aguila lager preferred by the North Americans.

They made small talk; the Americans wanted to know what a limey was doing down in the Amazon. 'Just a holiday; wanted to try that out-of-body experience thing, you know,' Hugh told them, while they offered the revelation that they were just exploring their 'back yard' and looking for some good weed.

The next morning, Ricaurte was waiting for them on the steps of the lodge, picking his remaining teeth with a small stick. 'Okay, you ready? We take boat now.'

They followed him through the sweltering streets to the river. There were few cars even on the main drag, just motorbikes buzzing in and out of the pedestrians. Leticia still had no roads in or out; the only way to get there was by air or river. Hugh bought a bag of buñuelos from a street vendor, small balls of deep-fried white cheese with salty flour, just in case.

An open canoe-like boat with an outboard motor was waiting for them, and they boarded gingerly, taking care not to tip it over and distributing their meagre belongings evenly around the sides.

'No swim, piranha!' Ricaurte told them cheerfully as they slid off into the brown water.

'Not to mention bilharzia,' muttered Hugh.

'What's that?' said the ponytail, slapping at a mosquito.

'Oh, nothing; nothing to worry about if you don't swim.'

After some twenty minutes moving in silence through the dense jungle, nothing to hear but the putt-putt of the motor and nothing to see except flashes of huge iridescent butterflies, they passed a village incongruously called Macedonia. A further fifteen minutes further on they hove to by the muddy riverbank and clambered up wooden planks to the shoreline, where three huts with hammocks outside stood waiting for them.

'Your house on the left; sleep in hammock,' Ricaurte told them. 'We eat soon, beans and rice, then tomorrow we go walk to ceremony.'

'Fuck this,' said the Canadian. 'Not sure I want to go through with it.'

Hugh was glad he'd bought his buñuelos.

CHAPTER EIGHT

A Political Awakening

Albert enjoyed working on construction sites; it was hard, but that stopped him thinking too much. He'd sworn never to live at home again, even though his father had by this time retired and bought a modest three-bedroom house near the old Arborfield army camp in Berkshire, where he had a ready fraternity of former army colleagues to play golf and drink beer with. Instead, Albert found a room to rent in central Reading, a nondescript town west of London.

He soon left the business of building flats behind and found employment instead on a new ring road being constructed for the town. Most of the rest of the team were itinerant Irish labourers. After some initial teasing about his size, they soon accepted him, and he enjoyed their uncomplicated company. His gang leader was a kindly whiskery man called Gerry with a gangling gait, who in the early days put Albert on teamaking duties to give him a rest several times a day. Then, to his delight, Albert graduated to steamroller operator, which had to be one of the coolest jobs on site.

During his first summer of freedom, in 1969, he went to his first and only music festival, at Plumpton racecourse near Lewes in Sussex.

He was joined by a former schoolmate called Neil; Neil also lived in Reading, with his parents, and they'd bumped into each other at a football game at Elm Park. They pitched their tent and queued to see the big bands; Pink Floyd, King Crimson, Yes and the Who were all there. Then they queued for food, and queued for the toilets, and got drunk and smoked some hashish, threw up and failed to get laid. The tent collapsed and by Monday they were back in Reading, exhausted, dishevelled and filthy. Albert's impression of the hippy revolution remained unchanged by the experience.

His mother, who he had continued to visit regularly when he knew his father would be at the golf club, contracted pneumonia about this time and died a slow death. She was buried in the village church in Arborfield. Thereafter he never visited home again, until it was time to bury his father in the same plot. Daphne, meanwhile, had emigrated to Australia on a ten-pound ticket and married an 'iron man' from the northwest, who earned a living scraping iron ore off mountains while she worked as a nurse in the unlikely-sounding town of Paraburdoo, and she failed to put in an appearance.

It was also around 1969 that Albert started to take an interest in politics – not in how he could take part in the process, but more in how he could help rip it apart. Despite his upbringing, or perhaps because of it, he was intensely proud of his country, and it pained him every time he had to put a new line through another country that was no longer part of the empire. He'd been born into the greatest empire the world had ever seen, but, in the short time between childhood and adulthood, it had all but disappeared, and it was getting smaller every year. At the same time, he resented what he saw as the 'invasion' of his country by immigrants from the former empire, many of them from the Indian subcontinent, but also from places such as the Caribbean, Ghana, Kenya and Nigeria.

The year before, he'd been captivated by Enoch Powell's famous speech attacking rising levels of immigration, especially from the Commonwealth. It had struck a chord with Albert, as many Asians were gravitating towards Reading and nearby Slough, seeking work in and around Heathrow airport, and he'd taken an instinctive dislike to them. He didn't even like curry. He was therefore stunned when Ted Heath sacked Powell as Shadow Defence Secretary the day after the speech. Everyone he knew supported Powell; even the polls showed massive support. Was that how democracy worked?

'I reckon Heath looks like a queer. He can never be PM; no one could trust him,' he told his workmates, none of whom really cared.

'It's all blather, Albert, boyo. None of them cares about us. They lives in their world and we lives in ours,' Gerry remarked. 'Now go and make some tea, and don't forget to warm the pot.'

The US war in Vietnam was also raging, along with the Biafran war in Nigeria. They were the first two widely televised wars in history; every day the public were treated to pictures of starving Biafrans and GIs getting blown to bits. The prime minister, Harold Wilson, decided to supply arms to the Nigerian army, while the French backed the Biafrans. Albert thought it was wrong that Wilson was backing a Muslim government against a Christian minority, and in the end some two million Biafrans starved to death with Wilson's help and desire to maintain a controlling access to the vast oil reserves in the Nigerian Delta region. It didn't seem right.

It was around the same time that Wilson decided Britain could no longer afford to offer defence to the Trucial States in the Arabian Gulf, even though they had just started to export oil. Sheikh Zayed, the ruler of Abu Dhabi, flew to London to plead with Wilson to change his mind, but the Labour leader was adamant, and ripped up a treaty that had been in place since 1892. The United Arab Emirates were born and announced their independence, along with Bahrain and Qatar, a few years before the huge extent of their oil and gas deposits and fabulous wealth became apparent. Although they had not technically been colonies – they were officially known as 'protectorates' – Albert still struck more angry lines through his list of former British 'possessions'.

Closer to home, Albert admired the methods, if not the ideology, of the Red Army Faction in Germany and Italy's Red Brigades, and the way they targeted politicians, industrialists and bankers, like modern-day Robin Hoods. But he knew too they would ultimately change nothing. The establishment would win, just as they would in Northern Ireland, where Wilson had ordered in the troops.

His biggest heroes, though, were the Great Train Robbers who, unarmed, gave the establishment an enormous poke in the eye, and hurt them where it hurt most – their dignity. When they took off with more than two million pounds they made a laughing stock of the government, which was their greatest crime, and which led them to being mercilessly hunted down and given sentences that not even a murderer would get.

Of course, to Albert's consternation, Edward Heath *did* become prime minister in 1970. Heath promptly decimalised the old currency and took the country into the European Economic Community, after a referendum which saw 67% of those who voted supporting the idea of joining the Common Market. No one suspected at the time that joining a trading bloc was to be the thin end of the wedge for the creation of a federal Europe and the loss of national sovereignty.

This was also about the time when Albert first started exploring political groups and attending their meetings, and the time when he met Annabelle, both of which would have a profound impact on his life.

CHAPTER NINE

Not an Out-of-Body Experience

'Happy New Year!' Hugh threw his bag onto the floor and gave his friend a bear hug, as much as a skinny guy can give a bear hug.

'Gerroff! What the fuck happened to you?' Miles pushed him away. Despite getting Hugh's postcard, he was still annoyed by the way his roommate had disappeared on him.

'Where do I begin? Colombia, what a fucking place, *fucking* being the operative word. Something of a disaster, really, but I guess I learned something… come on, let's get some food and beers in and I'm going to tell you all about it. And I'm sorry about the way I left, it was all kind of spur of the moment, but you got my postcard?'

'Yeah.' Miles shrugged, then smiled. 'All right, you old bastard, I forgive you. So, what's the story, then?'

Later that evening, sitting amid discarded pizza boxes and with cans of McEwan's Export in hand, Hugh recounted his adventure, from the time he was discovered in the strange woman's shop doorway to the moment he and his three companions were dumped by Ricaurte in their jungle hut.

'Well, we got our beans and rice, and then we were given a cup of milky coffee each. It tasted a bit strange, to be honest, but we didn't think much about it. Anyway, to cut a long story short, we slept, and we slept, and then we slept some more – and believe me, sleeping in a hammock isn't easy. When we finally woke up, everything was quiet, Ricaurte was nowhere to be seen… and nor were our belongings!'

'You were robbed?'

'Yes, everything was gone. They had us hook, line and sinker! I mean, I was lucky because I'd slept in my clothes with the money belt on – it had the last of my money, my passport and air tickets in it – but the others lost the lot, just had whatever they'd slept in.'

Miles was doubled over laughing now, holding his sides. 'Christ, they saw you coming! So what did you do?'

'The place was deserted, but eventually we managed to get help from a passing fisherman. I was the only one with money, but he was happy to take us back to Leticia for fifty bucks. Probably a month's wages for him.'

'What about the police?'

'Of course, we reported it, but they just shrugged. Maybe they were part of the scam; who knows? Anyway, there was nothing to be done except cut our losses and get the hell out of there. I left the Americans enough money for them to call home and get some money wired out, then headed for the airport. Fortunately, my tickets still worked, and a week later I was back in Blighty, wiser but poorer.'

'You're a mad bugger, you know that? So much for an out-of-body experience. Anyway, at least you're alive, and it was probably more interesting than stacking supermarket shelves, which is how I spent my holiday.'

Hugh reached for another beer and went to the window to light a cigarette. 'I did learn something, though.'

'Enlighten me.'

'That if you're an arsehole when you go to the Amazon, you'll still be one when you get there and still be one when you get back!' They both laughed this time and drank a toast. 'I also learned that you can't trust anyone.'

'Well, I suppose that should stand you in good stead if you make it into politics,' Miles told him, still shaking his head in mirth. 'Believe no one, especially other politicians!'

'Amen to that.'

*

The next day, Hugh returned to the little shop where his adventure had started, armed with a huge bunch of yellow roses and a box of chocolates.

Fiona opened the door and looked at him. She didn't seem in the least surprised to see him. 'Ach, it's you. I wondered when you'd be back.'

'What do you mean, you wondered when I'd be back?' Hugh asked as he stepped over the threshold, to be met by the smell of incense sticks.

Fiona took the flowers and busied herself arranging them in a vase, cutting off the stem bottoms. 'Ah, that's lovely, that is. What did I mean? I knew you were coming back, that's all. I read your tea leaves; you might remember I didn't use a strainer? I can "see" things, you know.'

'You read my tea leaves? Can you really do that?' Hugh was open-mouthed.

'So how was yer oot-of-body experience, then, if I might enquire?' Fiona cocked her head to one side as she looked at him.

'Er, well, not so much out of body; more out of brain, really,' Hugh confessed. He told her what had happened.

'Och, well, dinnae worry aboot it, but I can tell you that you have a bright future, lad.' Fiona's face creased into a smile, her eyes twinkling. 'And thanks for these beautiful flowers, they're grand.'

'Well, I hope so, but I think you should take that sign out of your window.'

CHAPTER TEN

A Secret Society

Annabelle. God, she was the most amazing person he had ever met. From the first, when he was with her, it was if there were tiny electric shocks running through his body.

Albert had by this time changed his name to Victor: V for violence, V for vengeance, V for vendetta. It just seemed to fit. Albert was a silly fucking name anyway, just like his sister's. Their parents must have been barking mad.

He'd also given up on the road building and started his own one-man loft conversion company, subcontracting the bulk of the work whenever he managed to secure any deals. He bought a Ford Transit van, painted a sign on the side saying, simply, *Vic's Loft Conversions*, and took out an advertisement in the yellow pages. In no time the business was rolling in, until he found himself employing a couple of labourers of his own.

He was currently in a packed meeting of the National Front, founded a few years earlier by AK Chesterton, cousin of the writer GK Chesterton. There were a lot of skinheads but also some older people, working people, not your average middle-class 'intellectual' types. With the country falling apart under first Wilson and now Heath, the National Front had struck a chord with many people, its membership surging above 20,000.

Victor, or Vic, as he preferred to be called, had been to a few of their meetings and liked what he heard, but he was careful not to join any of the right-wing political parties such as the White Defence League, the British Union of Fascists or the Greater Britain Movement. He was sure they were heavily infiltrated by the police, and to become a card-carrying member was to be identified. He preferred to stay in the shadows.

The guy on stage was raging about the country being stabbed in the back, warning the audience that they faced a future of civil unrest and interracial violence unless the flood of immigrants was stopped. The air was thick with cigarette smoke mixed with the sweat of three hundred or more bodies, and a roar of approval went up at every pause.

'They'll take your houses! They'll take your schools! Your children won't be safe!' the speaker bellowed. The crowd whooped and brayed, and the skinheads at the front in their Doc Marten boots, in some ways possibly the last hurrah of the white working class, were jumping up and down in unison and singing, 'We're going to bash a Paki, we're going to bash a Paki, la-la-la-la, la-la-la-la,' but Vic stayed standing quietly at the back of the hall.

Suddenly he had the strange sense that he was being watched, and turned quickly to his left to find himself facing a slim, dark-haired woman wearing black jeans and a black leather jacket, several feet away. She had no time to avert her gaze, so instead she gave him an inviting smile and moved to his side.

'You're very quiet,' she said as the noise of the crowd faded into the background. 'Are you a cop or something?'

'Am I *what*?' Vic burst out laughing. 'Oh, that's a good one, but no, I'm not. I'm just listening. I'm interested, up to a point.'

'I've heard it all before; it's pretty much the same every week. I'm Annabelle, by the way, and I could seriously do with a drink.'

Vic was stupefied. Since he had first been banished to boarding school, women had become something of a mystery to him, something to be lusted after or fantasised about, but not socially engaged. He'd had a few less-than-satisfactory one-night stands – getting sex wasn't difficult now that women were equating loads of sex with freedom and people like Germaine Greer were telling them all to burn their bras – plus an hour with a prostitute in a filthy massage parlour, but he'd almost stopped thinking about women as sentient beings; he'd forgotten how to approach them or talk to them. Now he stared at the apparition before him, the dark hair framing an oval face, that Mona Lisa smile, full lips slightly parted and painted a deep red, and a pair of eyes so dark they were almost black. And she was *talking* to him, teasing him, as if they really were from the same planet; as if they were just two human beings, equals, and sex had nothing to do with it. He shuddered as his spine tingled.

'Well? Cat got your tongue, has it?'

Vic coughed and tore his eyes away. 'No, I, er, I was just – yes, I'd love a drink! Look, I've got my car outside, I know a nice pub in Caversham – well, it's in Mapledurham, really; it's not far. Better than the centre of poxy Reading.'

Annabelle put her arm through his. 'Lead the way, then, Sir Lancelot!'

It was starting to drizzle, but Vic had parked his Ford Anglia less than twenty yards down the street. and they were soon inside. He tried to get it started, after flooding the engine on full choke in his flustered state.

'Who are you really?' Vic asked nervously as the engine finally coughed into life. 'I mean, I've never been picked up before. How do you know I'm not some sort of lunatic?'

'I can look after myself. Karate black belt, in fact, and I've got this.' She jerked her right arm forwards, and in her hand appeared a thin blade, a stiletto. 'I've been watching you for a while. You've been at a few of the meetings. I know who you are.'

'What the fuck?'

'All in good time, Vic, all in good time. Let's get to that pub.'

'How do you know my name?'

'Like I said, all in good time.'

They drove past Reading station, then snaked their way across Caversham Bridge and turned left up to the heights. Shortly after a sign announcing Mapledurham, Vic turned right and pulled up outside a pub called the Pack Saddle. 'I like this place. A bit old-fashioned, but it's out of the way, and the food is good, if you're hungry?'

'It's perfect. Let's get inside.'

They chose a table with a corner seat so they sat at right angles to each other. Annabelle ordered a half-pint of Guinness, while Vic got himself a pint of Greene King with a whisky chaser. He needed to calm down.

'Okay, so how about you tell me what this is all about?' he said as he put the drinks on the table.

'What happened to your eye?'

Vic's hand automatically went to his right eye. 'Childhood accident.'

He went on to tell her how he'd poked his own eye out, and now had a collection of glass eyes of different colours to suit his mood. Today he was wearing a pale green one, which almost matched the grey of his good eye. He also had a perfectly matching grey one, a brown one, a blue one, and a red one for when he wanted to be especially disconcerting.

Annabelle laughed, a deep throaty laugh which helped put Vic at ease, then put her cards on the table. She'd noticed him a couple of months earlier, she said, at a meeting of the British Movement, another one popular with the skinheads with whom Vic mingled at Reading FC's football matches. As for his name, well, she pointed out that it was painted on the side of his van. She told him she was looking for likely recruits for a new group: a very secretive one, but one that had big plans.

'And how do I know *you're* not a cop?' Vic asked.

'You don't, not yet, but a cop probably wouldn't do this.' She slid a hand under the table onto his inner thigh, then squeezed his rock-hard cock. 'It could be construed as entrapment.'

Vic gasped, nearly shooting his load, then took a big gulp of his beer. 'Okay, okay, let's say I believe you. What do you want?'

'So, I know you have a construction business; you're legit, mostly doing loft conversions or splitting up houses into tiny flats, I believe? It's a perfect cover; you pay your taxes, you work hard, you're below the radar.'

She went on to explain that theirs was a long-term plan to bring down the government, to pay the bastards back. The country was in a mess with the miners on strike and the three-day working week as Edward Heath desperately tried to save energy. The only solution was violence; the ballot box never solved anything, as the IRA knew.

As the evening wore on and they refilled their glasses and ordered fish and chips, Vic found himself agreeing with everything she said. He thought he might be in love, although he wasn't really sure what love was. 'So, what do you want me to do?'

'Nothing for now; just stay in touch. I want you to be a kind of sleeper. Talking of which?' She leaned back seductively.

It took him a moment to realise what she was suggesting, but he quickly recovered and invited her back to his small flat on the banks of the Thames, on the north side of Caversham Bridge. That night they had wild sex; she taught him things he'd not even imagined in his wildest dreams. He'd never known anything like it, and his life was never the same again.

CHAPTER ELEVEN

AN APPRENTICESHIP BEGINS

Hugh and Miles finished university and went their separate ways, but promised to stay in touch. Hugh had indeed decided to go into politics and, through family connections, managed to secure an internship at Westminster in the office of his local Conservative MP. Miles had opted to become a journalist and was accepted as an apprentice reporter on the *Reading Evening Post*, the first of the new breed of Thomson regional newspapers which employed computer-based web offset printing, instead of the traditional and more expensive hot metal press.

Before starting, Miles spent the summer at home in Cornwall. His mother, Molly, still lived in a small terraced fishing cottage in Lannanta, which the English call Lelant. Miles loved to lie in bed listening to the huge gulls screaming their defiance and anger at no one and nothing, before wheeling off to carpet bomb random parked cars with their incredibly corrosive excrement. If the wind was up, he could hear the sea rushing into the Heyl estuary from the North Atlantic.

He took a job as a lifeguard in the hut overlooking Porthkidney beach. It was a twenty-minute walk from his mother's house, past the small and very old church of St Uny and the Commonwealth war graves with their distinctive Celtic crosses, skirting the golf links with the Cornish flag flapping from the clubhouse, white cross on black background, then over the railway bridge and along the coastal path until he reached the lifeguards' lookout.

It was rarely busy, as there was no car access and most tourists were too lazy to walk the coastal path to get there. Quite a few who did make it were dog walkers, as it was one of the few permanently dog-friendly beaches on that stretch of coast. Through his binoculars he watched them scooping up their pets' poo in gaily coloured little plastic bags, which they toted around like trophies.

The beach was huge, the sea an amazing turquoise colour in the shallows, like a Caribbean beach, and a deeper blue farther out. In winter, beneath storm clouds, it would turn grey and be covered with white horses whipped up by the wind. At low tide, the sea was almost half a mile from his observation post, and he often wondered if he spotted someone in trouble, a board or kite surfer, how he would ever reach them in time to be of any use. Even a call to air sea rescue would be of dubious help.

Far to his right, he could see the sand bar where his father and uncle had perished when he was just twelve years old. There'd been a storm, and they had foundered on the treacherous bar trying to get back into Heyl port. He missed his father, but he didn't blame the sea; how could you? It was just the sea; it had to be treated with respect, and the storm that took his father and uncle was sudden and unexpected.

Above all, he loved this part of the country, with its rugged rocky coastline and pure salt air. Even the Edinburgh air had tasted stale by comparison, as if it had already been used, breathed in and out a million times. He couldn't imagine what it was like in really big cities like London, or, even worse, in inland places like Birmingham or Leeds. He'd never been to any of them, and had no real inclination to do so.

When he had time off, he'd borrow his mother's ancient Volvo, load up his surfboard and wetsuit and drive the few miles around the coast to Gwithian, which faced west, so the swell and waves were usually better. There he would spend hours in the water opposite the lighthouse with other surfers, many who he'd known since childhood, waiting for the dream ride.

It was a perfect summer, the sky invariably blue with only occasional wispy cirrus clouds far above, but the sea breeze was always there to keep the temperature at a manageable level. After work, unless he was having a few pints at the Badger Inn with old friends, he rarely went out.

Before university, outside the tourist season, he would sometimes take the coastal train along the clifftops to St Ives, just two stops away, for a nice restaurant meal. During the summer holidays, though, it was unbearable, the tiny streets crammed with grockles from all over the country, along with a surprising number of Germans. It seemed that millions of Germans were glued every week to some family drama set in Cornwall, like a kind of *Coronation Street* by the sea, and hundreds of thousands came to see what it was really like every summer.

Most evenings that summer Miles stayed at home with his mother, pottering in the tiny garden, which although small was home to a surprising number of plants, and doing odd jobs about the house. They would drink endless cups of tea and listen to the occasional play together on the radio.

Molly was a small, rotund woman with greying hair and red cheeks, and endlessly cheerful. She loved having her only son at home and would cook his favourite foods, such as roast lamb with new potatoes and fresh greens, or, if they were lucky, a rare Cornish sole fried in butter. For his part, he was content to be fussed over and enjoy her love and the peace and quiet, treasuring these moments together, not knowing how many more there might be. Since his father's death, he was acutely conscious of the transitory and unpredictable nature of life.

But all good things come to an end. Before he was ready August was over, and it was time for Miles to set off for his new life in Reading, a town he knew little about. Molly drove him to the station in nearby St Erth, which boasted trains to Reading, a four-and-a-half-hour journey at an eye-watering cost.

Emerging from a litter-strewn and depressing Reading station under overcast skies, and not knowing his way around, he took a taxi to his new digs, an equally depressing bedsit in Battle Street. It was near the old cattle market on the west side of the town, just beyond the new ring road. If he'd known, he could have walked it in less time than it took them to drive around the tortuous one-way system. But it was what it was, and he dumped his bag on the floor and lay down for a snooze before thinking about some food and his upcoming first day at work.

CHAPTER TWELVE

A Seat in Parliament

Hugh had an easier time of it. After a summer of leisure in the Lincolnshire countryside, attending point-to-point meetings and going to a variety of balls designed to pair off eligible daughters and sons, he finally drove his Triumph Herald down to London. His parents allowed him to set up shop in a small flat they owned in Pimlico, not far from the Tate gallery and an easy walk along the north bank of the Thames to Westminster.

He was excited. Although the local MP he was interned to was a stuffy old bore who rarely bothered to attend the Commons, especially as they were now the opposition party again, Hugh saw his internship as a stepping stone to great things. In fact, the less the sitting MP was around, the better from Hugh's point of view; it meant he got to attend functions in his employer's place and to indulge in some serious networking.

In some of his more fanciful moments, as Hugh admired himself in his grey Savile Row pinstripe suit with pale blue silk tie, he imagined the day when he would make his maiden speech as an MP himself, the house listening spellbound as he outlined his vision of the future. A future where three-day working weeks and blackouts were a distant memory, where Britain was once more the powerhouse of Europe, the envy of the world, prosperous, supreme and just.

In the meantime, he had to dodge piles of uncollected rubbish as the binmen had ceased work, the car industry was in crisis, the miners were on strike, inflation was through the roof, and Margaret Hilda Thatcher had toppled the creepy and embittered Edward Heath as leader of the Conservative opposition party. They were heady times.

The pipe-smoking Harold Wilson had suddenly announced his retirement in 1976, handing over the poisoned chalice of a minority government to James 'Sunny Jim' Callaghan. Callaghan staggered on as prime minister, propped up by the Liberal Democrats, better known as the limp dumbs.

It couldn't last, and it didn't. The UK lurched from one crisis to the next as inflation continued to soar and there was a run on the pound sterling. 'Red Robbo', AKA Derek Robinson, a lifelong member of the Communist Party, managed to lead more than 500 walkouts from British Leyland, despite it being nationalised and bailed out by the government while they produced crap cars such as the Austin Allegro, the Morris Marina and the Austin Princess.

Arthur Scargill was another Communist in the mining sector, a pint-sized Napoleon type of figure who was adept at picking the wrong fight at the wrong time. He had played a key role in the strikes which brought down the Heath government, but would go on to destroy the industry some years later when he came head-to-head with Thatcher. In Moscow they were rubbing their hands together with glee. Their money was being well spent.

It all came to a head in the 'Winter of Discontent', after striking tanker drivers were awarded a 13% pay rise. Health workers, rubbish collectors and gravediggers, amongst others, all demanded the same. When 'Sunny Jim' stepped off an aeroplane after a conference in the Caribbean looking suntanned and cheerful, the 'Currant Bun', sometimes also known as the *Sun* newspaper, ran its famous headline 'Crisis? What Crisis?' The prime minister never said it, but it caught the mood of the nation. When Thatcher tabled a motion of no confidence in Callaghan's government, she won with the support of minor parties, and went on to win the subsequent 1979 general election, the same year that the USSR invaded Afghanistan.

All of this was nectar to Hugh. His mentor resigned his seat, saying he'd 'never work for a bloody woman', and Hugh got to stand in his place and won his coveted seat in parliament. He really was now the honourable Hugh de Sommerville.

To top it all, Hugh had started walking out with a ravishing blonde who was a known socialite belonging to one of London's wealthiest families. Together they frequented some of the capital's most notorious nightclubs, and were a regular feature in the celebrity columns of the national newspapers and magazines. Life, it seemed, couldn't get much better, but it did.

Despite his social life, Hugh did take his work as an MP seriously, regularly championing the causes of his constituents, something for which they were duly grateful. Nor did he forget his friend Miles, who he would occasionally invite up to Marlow, midway between London and Reading on the banks of the Thames, for a sumptuous luncheon at the world-famous Compleat Angler restaurant. Miles wasn't particularly happy in Reading, which he described as a shabby town run by an inefficient Labour council, and Hugh was sympathetic.

'Get a job on the *London Evening Standard*,' he said. 'It'd be much more fun, and I know the editor; I can put in a word.'

Miles thanked him and said he'd think about it, as soon as he had finished his apprenticeship.

CHAPTER THIRTEEN

A Chance Encounter

Life was good for Vic as well. Business was booming, and he'd expanded into basement conversions to complement his loft work. He felt he was outgrowing Reading, and started eyeing the lucrative London market.

He'd also taken out a sizeable mortgage and swapped his modest flat for a spacious Victorian house on Caversham Heights with a view across the Thames. The garden ran down to the water, where he moored his new river cruiser.

He wasn't sure he'd ever had proper feelings for anyone apart from himself before, but that had changed with Annabelle. She'd left her job as a dentist's assistant and had become his office manager. Although she'd kept her own small flat in the centre of Reading, she spent most of her time at his house. They were blissfully happy there, mostly shunning the outside world, playing chess and Scrabble, enjoying barbecues in fine weather, drinking fine wines, and making their own plans. He hung on to her every word.

She'd ditched the black jeans and leather jacket look, and now dressed more conventionally in flowing designer dresses and coats, although always with flat-soled shoes. She couldn't abide high heels. But it didn't matter what she wore; she always looked stunning and sexy. Wherever they went, be it the boat races at Henley or racing at Newbury, she turned heads. Many of those staring wondered about the near-albino man with a glass eye at her side, and how on earth she had ended up with him.

'We need to appear respectable,' she told him. 'But we mustn't lose the anger. Above all, we mustn't get too comfortable and fall into the bourgeois trap and forget where we are coming from. We mustn't forget the endgame and what we really want to achieve. The rest is just window dressing.'

As the months went by, she introduced him to other members of her group, such as it was. Mostly they met the others one by one in different pubs, never at the house, although sometimes up to five or six of them would hold a picnic in a public park, well away from prying ears and eyes, where they would discuss their plans. At these events, no one gave their real names, nor any clue as to their real identities. Only Annabelle seemed to possess all of their contact numbers, and at the meetings she always wore a blond wig, dark sunglasses and a headscarf. Vic rarely attended, but when he did, he wore dark shades to hide his glass eye, a light ginger hairpiece and a pork pie hat.

The rest were divided into cells of two. Even three was felt to pose a danger; as the old saying went, 'two's company, three's a crowd'. They were a mixed bunch, some young and full of the kind of anger Vic had felt at their age, others middle-aged but with a quiet determination. They all agreed, though, that society was broken and needed a reset, something that could only be achieved through direct action.

One evening in late December, Vic was walking down King Street in the commercial centre of Reading, where'd he been to buy Annabelle a Christmas present, a delicate white gold necklace with a seahorse and a single emerald eye. He'd never bought anyone a Christmas present before; not since he was a child, at least, when he was obliged to get something or other to put under the tree for his parents and sister. He wondered if he'd gone over the top.

As he turned towards the station car park where he'd left his Rover 80, a major upgrade from his old Ford Anglia, he suddenly saw a young man being set upon by a group of Asian youths. There were three of them against one. The victim had his back to the wall and was giving a good account of himself, but the odds were not in his favour; he'd be overwhelmed sooner rather than later.

A red mist descended on Vic, and he felt all the old rage well up as he roared in fury and piled in. The assailants were taken by complete surprise as Vic's fists flailed left and right. Small and scrawny he might have been, but his aggression was phenomenal. Blood was already pouring from the nose of one of the attackers, and another staggered back as Vic caught him with a right hook and kicked him in the balls, leaving him doubled over. The three ran, as much as they still could, two of them dragging the one Vic had kicked.

'You all right, mate?' Vic asked, breathing heavily. 'Haven't enjoyed myself so much in a long time!'

The young man had a cut above his left eye but otherwise seemed unharmed. 'Yes, thanks, thank you very much. Don't know where you came from, but I owe you fucking big time.' He was also out of breath, leaning forwards, hands on thighs. 'Thought I was in big trouble there.' He held out a hand. 'Miles, Miles Blincow.'

'Vic. Don't mention it. Come on, I'll buy you a pint and you can tell me all about it.'

He led Miles to the station car park and opened the door of his Rover, and they sank into the luxurious leather seats. It was a bit of an antique, having been out of production for more than ten years, but it was a beautiful car, with a walnut dashboard, disc brakes front and rear, and a powerful engine.

'They don't make 'em like this any more,' Vic said. 'She's a beauty; wouldn't swap her for any of the modern crap. Now sit back and relax. We'll go and pick up my woman, and then go somewhere nice and get to know each other.'

Miles did as he was told, leaning back and holding a handkerchief to his cut. He marvelling at the comfort and smoothness of the ride as they drove, glancing left towards the *Evening Post*'s main offices as they approached Caversham Bridge.

They stopped briefly outside Vic's impressive home, where he sounded the horn, and Annabelle came out to join them. It had started to rain.

'Hello, love, this is Miles; bit of a long story, Miles, this is Bella, she's my soulmate. No, don't get up; Bella can sit in the back. Never like a stranger sitting behind me, and I don't know you yet, so you're still a stranger.'

Ten minutes later they were sitting by a roaring fire in the Pack Saddle. Vic fetched two pints of ale for himself and Miles, and a glass of chilled chardonnay for Annabelle.

'Been in a bit of a punch-up,' he told Annabelle, dumping a couple of packets of crisps and one of pork scratchings on the table. 'Saw Miles here being set on by a bunch of Pakis and weighed in, gave them a right good kicking. So, what's the story, Miles, old cocker?'

Miles took a long drink from his glass, glad to note that he'd stopped shaking, and smiled. 'Well, I don't know that they were Pakistanis, but given the story, because it was about a story, I suspect they were.'

'Now, don't get us wrong, mate,' Vic interjected. 'We've got nothing against anyone because of their skin colour, and anyway they're all different. Take the Sikhs, for example; top guys, they are – well, most of them – and good workers. I employ a couple, as it happens. Not so keen on your Pakistani, to be honest, or the Hindu, while the Jamaicans are fucking useless except for their music. I mean, look at those fucking riots in Brixton, Christ, a hundred vehicles torched in a day and dozens of shops, and for what? 'Cause a cop was trying to help a stabbed black kid, and the mob thought he was being arrested; least that's what I heard. But they are what they are. Trouble is, there are too many of them coming over, and they don't mix; they're different to us. I mean, I couldn't care less what they get up to in their own countries, but they want to bring their ways here, they don't accept our ways, and that can't be right. Sorry, I'm ranting. You were saying?'

Miles was fascinated by Vic's eyes. He'd realised by now that one of them was glass, but, while Vic's good eye was a greenish-grey, the glass one he was wearing today was bright blue, a complete mismatch. He tried not to stare. 'Well, the thing is, I'm a reporter.'

'A reporter?' said Annabelle, glancing at Vic.

'Yes, with the *Evening Post*. I just finished my apprenticeship. Anyway, I did this story about hygiene in some of the local restaurants, all kinds, Italian, English, French, whatever, and some of them were pretty filthy, to be honest. But a couple of the curry houses were especially bad, and next thing I knew the council inspectors had closed them down. Found mouse droppings, contaminated meat, the lot. So I suspect tonight was my payback.'

'Fuck me,' said Vic, helping himself to a handful of pork scratchings. 'Old Enoch was right, you know.'

'Tell me about being a reporter,' Annabelle said as she drained her glass.

'How about a refill first?' Miles suggested, but Vic stopped him as he was about to get up, putting a hand on his arm.

'You just sit back and relax; this is on us.' He signalled the barman to get another round in. 'Put it on the slate, Jim.'

Miles told them he was from Cornwall, that he'd just served his three-year apprenticeship as a reporter on the *Evening Post*, and that it had mostly been pretty tedious stuff. Magistrates' court, parish council meetings, ambulance chasing to car crashes or fires.

'The parish council meetings are the worst. I tend to fall asleep in them. Fell off my chair once, and the council chairman complained to the editor; he gave me a right rollicking.' He laughed, and Vic and Annabelle joined him. 'The restaurant thing was my first investigative job. I thought it was a good piece, but looks like not everyone agreed.'

'Where does that name come from, then?' Vic abruptly changed the subject. 'Blincow, you said it was, ain't that right?'

'Well, it seems one of my ancestors had a blind cow, and the rest of the village called them the blind cow people. Eventually it got shortened to Blincow,' Miles explained.

'No way!'

'Yeah, that's bollocks, actually, I've no idea where it comes from, Cumbria, apparently, but one of them must have ended up in Cornwall, and we're still there. Apart from my dad; he died in a fishing accident, got caught in a storm.'

'That's sad,' Annabelle said.

'Yeah, I still miss him, but my mum's still down there, and I go down whenever I can.'

'So, what now?' Annabelle asked. 'Now that you've finished your apprenticeship? Is Reading the height of your ambition?' She arched an eyebrow. She was quite something, Miles thought, with her sleek black hair, black jeans and black polo-necked sweater under a long red raincoat.

'No, three years in Reading is more than enough. I don't really like it here. I live in a shithole of a bedsit. I think I'll go to London; that's where all the action is, after all. Eventually I'd like to be a foreign correspondent. Specifically, a war correspondent. But that would take time. Still, got to start somewhere.'

'London?'

'Yeah, the *Evening Standard*. I've applied for a job there. I've got a mate who's an MP and he knows the editor, so fingers crossed.'

'A mate who's an MP? *Evening Standard*?' Annabelle looked towards Vic, and gave him a discreet kick under the table.

'How come you know an MP?' Vic asked, on cue.

'We were at university together, in Edinburgh. I mean, we're very different, but we kind of bonded and shared digs. He's the MP for somewhere in Lincolnshire, a Tory, and we stay in touch. He arranges for us to meet for lunch every month or two.'

'Well, fuck me again, 'scuse my French,' said Vic. 'Tell you what, I scratched your back tonight, so to speak; maybe you can scratch mine in return. I've been thinking of expanding into London. Maybe you can help me?'

'Of course, if I can.'

They'd finished their drinks again. 'Come on,' Vic said, 'let's go back to our place and get something to eat.'

Back at the house, Annabelle quickly rustled up some scrambled eggs and a salad. She opened a bottle of wine, a fine Cheval Blanc, which Miles thought a bit incongruous to be drinking with scrambled eggs; although he was no wine expert, he knew this stuff didn't come cheap. He was also in awe at the deep pile carpets, the big television, the ultra-modern turntable with huge speakers, and the paintings on the walls.

Vic put on a Doors album while they ate, and told Miles about his work: how he did a lot of loft and house conversions, turning one-family homes into several flats, and more recently his move into basement conversions.

'The job I'm really after, though, is to get some of the maintenance work at Westminster,' he concluded. 'They put stuff out to tender every now and again, and I want to put in a bid. But I know how these things work; it's all about who you know, not what you know. So maybe you could get your chum to put in a word for me?'

Miles said he'd try; he'd need to know a lot more and he wasn't sure how much influence Hugh had, but it was worth a shot. Shortly afterwards, Vic drove him back to Battle Street.

'You're right. It is a shithole,' Vic said when he saw the house where Miles had his bedsit. 'But listen, stay in touch; you never know…'

CHAPTER FOURTEEN

A Rising Star

As it happened, Hugh was starting to have quite a lot of influence. He was a natural in the Thatcher government and quickly rose through the ranks to become a junior minister in the Home Office, tasked with helping to cull the bloated Civil Service, a job which he carried out with relish and efficiency. Like Thatcher, who he and his colleagues affectionately called Maggie, although not to her face, he was an arch believer in small government and allowing people to be self-reliant, rather than having a nanny state that reached into every nook and cranny of people's lives.

On the walls of his office, he had two of his favourite quotes from Churchill framed. *Socialism is the philosophy of failure, the creed of ignorance and the gospel of envy,* declared one, and *For a nation to try to tax itself to prosperity is like a man standing in a bucket and trying to lift himself up by the handle,* said the other. He also had one of Maggie's, which read, *The problem with socialism is that you eventually run out of other people's money.*

Arthur Scargill and Red Robbo weren't the only ones to make the mistake of taking on the Iron Lady, a title given to Thatcher in mockery by the Soviet army's *Red Star* newspaper, but which she had thrown back in their faces by adopting the sobriquet with pride. As her popularity began to nosedive amid economic gloom in 1982, the Argentinian dictator General Galtieri, whose own economy was also in freefall and under international pressure over his human rights abuses, decided to boost his own poll ratings. He invaded the Falkland Islands on the second of April, never guessing that within three days Thatcher would have cobbled together and dispatched a task force to retake them. The Argentinian surprise was understandable, given that the British Foreign and Commonwealth Office had been ready to cede the islands since 1965, seeing the British dependent territories of the Falklands and South Georgia as a barrier to better trade with South America.

Across the UK, pubs, streets and houses were awash with Union Jacks as everyone held their breath, watching the task force inch its way towards the South Atlantic. The Americans were aghast. General Galtieri was their kind of man, but then so was General Pinochet in Chile, and he was backing the Brits.

'Cheeky buggers. What do the Argies think they're playing at?' Hugh remarked to a colleague at the subsidised bar in Westminster.

'Do you think Maggie will actually go through with it?' his colleague replied.

'I don't *think*; I *know*. Our boys will give them a short, sharp shock and send them running off back to Buenos Aires with multiple fleas in their ears. Mark my words!'

He was right, but it was a close-run affair, with no thanks to the BBC. The main landings in the west of the Falklands were not going well, under constant air attack. A victory was required, and it was decided that 2 Para would launch a surprise attack on Goose Green in the east under Lieutenant Colonel Herbert Jones, who had to march his men for two days from San Carlos Bay. Imagine, then, Jones' surprise when he turned on his radio on the 26th of May to hear the BBC's World Service announcing the 'surprise' attack to the world. The element of surprise had been lost, but incredibly the Argentinians didn't take the report seriously and their troops in Goose Green relaxed.

Jones swore he would sue the BBC for treason after the war, but by the time the Argentinians at Goose Green surrendered on Argentine National Army Day three days later, Jones was among the eighteen British fatalities.

A couple of weeks later, the main Argentinian force around the capital, Port Stanley, also surrendered, leaving 649 of their own dead, along with 255 British. It was a resounding triumph for Thatcher and changed Britain's image around the world. The

Foreign and Commonwealth Office's concerns notwithstanding, other countries started taking Britain seriously again for the first time in years, and business with South America got a shot in the arm.

Thatcher's popularity at home recovered and she was returned to power with a landslide victory the following year. Galtieri, who was not so lucky, was quickly toppled, and civilian rule restored. Britain was suddenly bursting with pride, even if the Argentinians continued to burn with resentment.

'Bastards should be grateful; it's thanks to Maggie that they finally got rid of their military dictatorship,' Hugh told Miles as they shared a celebratory lunch in the Gay Hussar in Soho.

'Hmm, not sure they see it that way. Probably a lot of wounded pride.'

'Well, fuck 'em.' Hugh shrugged as he tucked into his stuffed cabbage with sour cream. 'Did you know this used to be Michael Foot's favourite haunt?'

'Yeah, I know. Not been here before. It's a bit old-fashioned, but got to say the food is good.' Miles was eating chicken paprika. 'Hungarian, isn't it?'

'Mm. So, tell me about the new job.'

'It's okay. Still finding my feet, trying to stay away from the court cases. It's better than Reading, but it's still a London newspaper, and I'm more interested in foreign news. I might try my luck at the *Guardian*, see if they have any openings.'

Hugh poured some more wine for each of them. It was a heavy Hungarian red. 'The *Guardian*, eh? They're a bit up themselves, if you ask me. I reckon you should check out the *Telegraph*, bigger budget, more foreign correspondents – and I know the editor.'

Miles laughed. 'Here we go again! I can't rely on you for all my jobs, and anyway I need to put in some time at the *Standard* before moving on, otherwise people won't take me seriously.'

'They will if you can break a couple of good stories. I might have something for you.'

CHAPTER FIFTEEN

A Pub Lunch

Annabelle and Vic met Hugh in slightly less salubrious surroundings, the Telegraph pub on Putney Heath. It was Wimbledon fortnight, and Hugh and his blonde bombshell, Sophie, had Centre Court tickets, courtesy of her multimillionaire industrialist father. Their relationship was getting a bit fractious, and Hugh was happy to leave her with her friends at the All England tennis club for a couple of hours while he went to meet Annabelle and Vic at Miles' request.

Given its position, surrounded by greenery and trees, the Telegraph had huge potential, but it was rundown and shabby, its cavernous interior poorly lit. Chairs were ripped, the stuffing bursting out, dirty and uninviting. Dogs lay about, panting, while their owners sipped from pint glasses of Guinness and London Pride. But it was discreet, which suited Hugh.

'Good of you to come.' Vic held out his hand for Hugh to shake, then introduced Annabelle. Hugh thought she was gorgeous, but inscrutable behind her dark sunglasses and straw boater hat. She wore a pair of bright yellow slacks, an ivory blouse and canvas shoes. Vic, on the other hand, was dressed in blue jeans and a chequered flannel shirt with work boots, and was throwing off his usual nervous energy. Like many before him, Hugh wondered what they saw in each other.

'No problem,' Hugh said. 'Always happy to help a friend of Miles, if I can.' Miles had warned him about Vic's eye, and he avoided staring at the brown glass one he was wearing today, a shocking contrast to his grey good eye.

They ordered drinks: a London Pride for Vic, white wine spritzer for Annabelle and an extra spicy Bloody Mary for Hugh. 'Bit of a hangover,' Hugh explained. 'With a bit of luck this might help, hair of the dog and all that. Plus the tennis is driving me slightly bonkers, to be honest.' They also ordered food: a burger for Vic, and Caesar salads with anchovies for Hugh and Annabelle.

They sat at a bench outside under the shade of an ancient cedar tree, well away from any of the other customers, and Vic outlined his plans and hopes, punctuated by the occasional thud of leather on willow as a couple of local amateur cricket teams battled it out on the nearby green.

'So, what do you think?' Vic concluded. 'Any chance you can put a word in? Have I missed anything out?'

'No, all seems pretty clear,' Hugh told him, finishing off his salad and draining the last of his Bloody Mary. 'Look, it's not really my bailiwick, but I'll ask around, find out who's in charge of this kind of thing. Probably some kind of bloody committee, but then there's always a head honcho. Trouble is, some of them don't do something for nothing, if you get my drift.'

'Yeah, I get it. Not really into bribes and suchlike; it always ends in tears.' Vic shrugged.

'Well, it wouldn't be anything so blatant as that. More than anything, whatever committee it is would have to be convinced that they're giving the contract to the right people. But you might need to hire some consultants, at least. You know, to lobby the right people?'

'Consultants! Bleeding parasites... I know a good joke about them. But some other time, maybe?'

Hugh gave Vic his card and they made their farewells, Vic promising he'd contact the MP with some follow-up.

'Seemed all right to me. Nice enough bloke,' Vic said as they filtered onto the M4 to make their way back to Reading.

'He's a politician,' Annabelle observed. 'Not to be trusted.'

'Well, sure, there is that, but as politicos go, he didn't seem too bad.'

'He's still a fucking politician.' She leaned back and closed her eyes.

'Yeah, all right,' Vic grunted, as he gunned the Rover into the outside lane, cruising at the maximum allowed speed.

CHAPTER SIXTEEN

A Scoop

The 'something' that Hugh had told Miles he might be able to provide as an exclusive was explosive, to say the least. According to Hugh, the Central Policy Review Staff, the CPRS, had been asked to come up with radical solutions to the burgeoning welfare state. It had been discussed at a special half-day cabinet meeting, and the proposals put forward included a freeze on welfare benefits, plans to charge for state education, an insurance-based health service, and a massive scaling back of public services.

'The chancellor is the driving force behind it, not Maggie,' Hugh told Miles.

'Geoffrey Howe?'

'The very one. But if my name gets out as the leak, I'm toast, so not a word.'

'A reporter never reveals his sources,' Miles said. 'And anyway, I need to dig around a bit first to back this up. In the end, you won't even be the source.'

Thatcher herself had still not managed to shake off the unwanted nickname of 'Milk Snatcher', having stopped the provision of free milk to primary school children as Education Secretary under Heath in 1970. If she was now seen as wanting to dismantle the welfare state, she could also be toast.

Miles was still relatively new at the *Standard*, and realised he didn't have the contacts required to back his story up. He decided to approach the senior political editor and explain he had a massive story, but he needed help.

'What massive story?' The political editor stubbed out another cigarette in his already overflowing ashtray. He was a cadaverous man in his fifties, with swept-back grey hair, a nicotine-stained moustache and a razor-sharp mind. He looked up at Miles over his half-moon spectacles and rammed another unwanted story on the spike, which was nearly full.

'It's delicate, but I can vouch for the information. But if we break the story, I want a shared byline at the least.'

'A shared byline? With me? Cheeky young sod, you're still wet behind the ears.'

'Suit yourself, forget I ever said anything,' Miles said, holding his ground and the other man's gaze. 'But if another paper breaks this before us, and they will, you'll be the one regretting it.'

The political editor leaned back and lit another cigarette, still glaring at Miles. 'You really are a cheeky fucker, but fair enough; I like a man who stands up for himself. So, agreed. If it's as good as you say, you can have your byline. But only if it's that good.'

'Great, that's great, I appreciate it, and you won't be disappointed, I promise you. But I can't tell you here. Can we go somewhere else? Preferably outside?'

The old hack glanced at his watch. 'Nearly twelve. Fancy a kebab? I know a nice little Turkish place, not far.'

'Sure, anything is fine by me.'

'Come on, then, an early lunch it is. Miles, isn't it? You're new here, aren't you?'

Fifteen minutes later they were sitting down in a snug Turkish restaurant with rugs on the walls and Turkish folk music playing softly from the wall-mounted loudspeakers, each with a glass of watered raki. The political editor, whose name was Don, ordered a kebab with a side salad, while Miles went for the kofta, lamb meatballs in a rich gravy.

'Enjoy, don't be shy, it's on expenses,' Don said. 'So, try me.'

Miles outlined what he'd been told, while Don listened intently.

'Bloody hell, that *is* massive,' Don said at last, sitting back. 'Could be a huge coup. What's your source?'

'That I can't tell you, but it's solid, from the horse's mouth, so to speak. But that's why I need you; you've got the better contacts in

Westminster. I need you to get some kind of confirmation that this is real, to protect my own source.'

'Makes sense. Sound thinking, in fact. Good God, I've suddenly lost my appetite. I want to get on with this pronto, because if anyone else gets a sniff, we're buggered.' He graciously raised his glass. 'I thank you, young sir. If this works out, I owe you one. You'll go far!'

It took Don just two days working all his contacts to confirm at least a watered-down version of what had been talked about with the CPRS in cabinet. Under intense questioning and not a little wine to loosen tongues, more than one minister admitted that 'something along those lines' had been discussed. The proposed freeze on welfare benefits, an end to state-funded higher education and an insurance-based health service were confirmed. It was enough to go on.

The *Evening Standard* splashed the story across its front page, and Miles got his promised byline. Other newspapers rushed to catch up.

The government, and Thatcher especially, were appalled. A leak like this had been the prime minister's greatest fear, and she quickly distanced herself from the story, saying there had been a 'riot' in cabinet and nothing was being planned to cut the welfare state. At the Conservative Party conference she announced that 'The NHS is safe with us,' a mantra every aspiring Conservative prime minister has felt obliged to repeat ever since. Thanks to her continuing popularity following the Falklands War, she got away with it.

CHAPTER SEVENTEEN

An Unforeseen Fall

Thatcher also got away with it when the IRA bombed a Conservative Party conference in Brighton in 1984, although five others were killed, including the deputy chief whip, Sir Anthony Berry, and more than thirty were injured. The bomb itself had been planted weeks before on a delayed timer in room 629, five floors above Thatcher's suite, but was somehow missed by police sniffer dogs.

Hugh was in the Grand Hotel when the bomb went off shortly before 3am, but, as luck would have it, he was still in the bar, doing his drunken and unsuccessful best to chat up an attractive young Tory campaign manager.

Like Hugh, the prime minister herself was also still awake and working on her conference speech in the sitting room of her suite. Had she been in the bathroom, it would have been another story, but the sitting room and bedroom were largely undamaged, and she and her husband Dennis were helped from the wreckage by rescue workers.

'Absolute cowardly bastards,' Hugh told Miles, who was also in Brighton to cover the conference. Since the story on plans to cut the welfare state, Miles had been taken under Don's wing, and had been promoted to assistant political editor.

'I never really thanked you for my big scoop,' Miles said. 'Often wondered why you did it.'

'The wets needed their wings clipped,' Hugh replied with a shrug, referring to the liberal wing of the Tory party. 'Howe was getting too big for his boots.'

'Right. The wets. We need to talk more about that.'

'Some other time, mate, not right now.' It was the day after the bomb, and Hugh was still shaken, but resolute. 'We'll hunt them down, you know. We'll get them, whatever it takes.'

'They've probably buggered off back to Ireland,' Miles observed between sips of his pint.

'They could go to China, for all I care. We'll still get them,' Hugh assured him.

And they did, tracking down the bomber, Patrick Magee, in Glasgow months later, and using a fingerprint from his hotel registration card to win a conviction.

Just weeks later, during an especially cold December, Thatcher held her historic meeting with the leader of the Soviet Union, Mikhail Gorbachev, at Chequers, the prime minister's country residence. She later told the world 'I like Mr Gorbachev. We can do business together.' The Russians were using her to sound out the Americans; they didn't feel comfortable approaching Washington DC directly, but knew that Thatcher and President Reagan were very close. After the Chequers meeting, Thatcher flew to China, Hong Kong, Honolulu and Camp David within six days, and at Camp David gave Reagan a full debrief about her talks with Gorbachev.

At home, however, Britain was riven by the miners' strike, with violent confrontations across the country as Scargill deployed flying pickets to try to stop all pits working. It was the most bitter dispute in British industrial history, and was enough for many on the left to applaud the IRA's Brighton attack. Scargill's big mistake, though, was not to bother to ballot members of the miners' union on strike action, and many, especially in the Midlands, worked throughout the dispute. It was nothing short of a power struggle between the unions and the government, and after a year the strike collapsed and Thatcher had scored another decisive victory.

In the coming years, on the international stage, Thatcher went from strength to strength. In 1987 she accepted Gorbachev's invitation to visit Moscow, when she wowed Muscovites after being given permission to meet people in the street without restrictions, and gave a blunt television interview in which she expressed exactly what she thought about communism.

She then spoiled it all by scoring a massive own goal when she introduced the poll tax. Intended to replace property rates, the poll tax was a flat rate tax on every adult in a property, rather than a tax based on the estimated value of a property. It was patently unfair, and sparked huge demonstrations. There were so many defaulters and people refusing to register that councils couldn't even collect the tax, the police hated it, and the Labour Party vowed to abolish it and saw their ratings soar. The clouds were gathering.

Hugh had caught Thatcher's eye and had been appointed as an assistant to the now foreign secretary, Geoffrey Howe, who was becoming distrusted by the prime minister. Part of Hugh's job was to keep an eye on him.

They witnessed the fall of the Berlin Wall, the collapse of communism across Eastern and Central Europe, and the flight of tens of thousands of easterners to the west. Hugh wondered what forces had been unleashed and how they would impact the rest of Europe. A united Germany would be a force to be reckoned with.

The wets were gaining influence, most prominent among them Geoffrey Howe, Jim Prior, Peter Walker and Lord Carrington. They hadn't dared move against Thatcher as long as her popularity ensured their jobs by winning elections, but the poll tax had changed that. They opposed many of her more hardline policies, but especially her stance on Europe.

Thatcher was an unashamed nationalist, proud of her country and its traditions. Some years earlier, despite fierce resistance from Brussels, she had drastically reduced Britain's contribution to the EU budget, and she was resolutely opposed to the creation of a federal Europe, believing that a free trade zone was quite enough. She was open about her fear of the country being swamped by alien cultures, while others in her cabinet were equally open about their support for more immigration.

Howe especially was passionately pro-Europe, and clashed with Thatcher when she strongly opposed joining the European Exchange Rate Mechanism, or ERM, even if the move was forced through a year before she felt compelled to step down. History was to prove her right, but the vultures were closing in. She sacked Howe, and he responded by attacking her in his resignation speech to the House of Commons, even going so far as to suggest it was time for a change of leadership.

The vainglorious Michael Heseltine, he of the lion's mane hairstyle, put himself forward to challenge Thatcher for the leadership of the party – and lost. But it wasn't a crushing defeat. Thatcher hadn't won by enough to avoid a second round of voting, and her authority was damaged.

The ineffectual ginger-headed leader of the opposition Labour Party, Neil Kinnock, called for a general election and tabled a vote of no confidence in the government. He lost as well – he never seemed to win anything – but Thatcher realised she'd lost the support of her cabinet and resigned late in 1990, just a month after the reunification of Germany, making an emotional exit from number 10 Downing Street.

She had been in power for eleven and a half years and had changed the face of Britain, from a workshy strike-ridden country into an economic powerhouse with a huge increase in home ownership. Two weeks later, Queen Elizabeth II bestowed upon Thatcher the Order of Merit, an honour given at the sole discretion of the monarch, which hardly supported rumours spread by Thatcher's enemies that the two women disliked each other.

The insipid and uninspiring John Major was appointed prime minister in Thatcher's place, and Hugh's star shone less brightly, then dimmed even further in the years to come. He had to be patient.

CHAPTER EIGHTEEN

THE GREY MAN

'Fucking John Major! I mean, what an absolute twat, and a traitorous one at that. Needs to be introduced to some piano wire if you ask me!' Vic fumed as he threw his newspaper to the floor and lay back on the white leather sofa.

'I didn't ask you,' Annabelle pointed out through the serving hatch from the kitchen. 'But you've got a point. Politicians never seem to do what people want them to do. It's as if they're taking orders from someone else, and lining their own pockets, of course. Which is why we have to deal with them in the only way that makes sense.'

'I mean, who needs a traffic cones hotline? Is that the best he can do?'

'I think you're missing the bigger picture, my love,' Annabelle told him.

'Eh? What do you mean?' Vic struggled up into a sitting position. 'Any chance of a small whisky and water? I need a drink.'

Annabelle duly served him a weak Scotch and water, no ice. Outside it was overcast and it looked like rain. Below them, on the river, a pair of swans paddled gracefully.

'Amazing how they mate for life,' Vic observed. 'Not like humans – ourselves excepted, of course.'

'The bigger picture,' Annabelle said patiently, 'is that the pound has just crashed, George Soros has made himself a billionaire by betting against the Bank of England, and we've crashed out of the ERM. But that's probably the good news; getting out of the ERM, I mean.'

'Yeah, right, how is that good news?'

'It keeps us at arms' length from those bastards in Brussels. The EU was always plan B for the Nazis if they lost the war, you know.'

Vic stood up and went to the window, knocking back the last of his drink and thinking about another. 'You are a genius, you know? It's why I'm mad about you. But what do you mean about that plan B stuff?'

'Okay, five-minute lesson.' Annabelle flicked the kitchen towel she was holding over her shoulder. 'Then I need to cook. Spag bol, your favourite, okay?'

'Okay, I'm listening.'

Annabelle started counting off on her fingers. 'One, Walter Hallstein, big honcho in the EEC. Two, Adolf Heusinger, head of the NATO Military Committee. Three, Kurt Waldheim, Secretary-General of the United Nations. All committed Nazis. You getting the picture?'

'I guess.'

'They control the EEC; they want a federal Europe. It's a German construct, conquest by another name. You don't eradicate evil with a few treaties and pieces of paper. A leopard doesn't change his spots and all that. And the frogs, don't even talk about them; they just carry on hanging on to the Hun's coattails. Now, I'm going to finish dinner. Open some wine, will you?'

'Right, right, never thought about it like that. How do you know all this stuff?' Vic muttered. 'Red or white?'

'I read a lot. And red. A good one!'

Vic descended to his treasured wine cellar and pulled out a bottle of 1972 Margaux. 'Not a bad year,' he said to himself. 'Needs to breathe a bit.'

Over dinner they continued their conversation. 'So why did we ever join the EU, then?' Vic asked. 'What's in it for us?'

'We joined in 1973; the EEC, anyway. It was Heath's way of trying to dig us out of the economic mire. It was known as the Common Market then, so a free trade area, but they always had plans to turn it into a federal state. And us joining meant we shafted all our old friends in Australia, New Zealand, Canada and so on.'

'Seems to cost us a fortune, too. Aren't we the biggest contributor?'

'Second biggest, after Germany, thanks to Maggie; she got us a rebate. But the Krauts seem to get a lot more out of it, and they control it, like I said. Pity de Gaulle isn't still around.'

'Old big nose? What do you mean?'

'As long as he was around, he kept blocking British membership. Saw us as a Trojan Horse for the Yanks. He was probably right, but then he never forgave us for winning the war for him anyway.' Annabelle twirled spaghetti around her fork and smiled seductively across the table.

'You know, I reckon if we'd never joined the shitfest that was World War One,' Vic said out of nowhere, 'the Huns would have taken France, or most of it anyway. There would have been no Weimar Republic, no Nazi party, and so no World War Two. We could have probably kept most of our empire too, or carved up Europe between us and the Krauts. They're kind of our cousins anyway.'

'You have a point there,' Annabelle said. 'Never mind de Gaulle, anyway. You wouldn't expect anything else from a frog, our oldest enemies and all that; what we need to worry about are the traitors in our own midst. And never mind traffic cones; what's important is that Major has just sold this country down the river with the Maastricht Treaty. I mean, "shared European citizenship"? A common currency? I mean, what the fuck has someone in Newcastle got in common with someone in Naples?'

'I like the cartoons of him with his underpants on the outside of his trousers. He's the original grey man,' Vic interrupted.

'The point is,' Annabelle continued, 'if that isn't federalism, I don't know what is. It's time we took some affirmative action. Enough of the sitting around and talking about it.'

'What did you have in mind?'

CHAPTER NINETEEN

A Taste of War

While Hugh's star was waning, at least temporarily, that of Miles was rising spectacularly. He'd outgrown the *Evening Standard* and landed his coveted job on the *Daily Telegraph*. Hugh had been right; they had a bigger budget than the left-wing *Guardian*, sold more newspapers, and had a good-sized foreign desk.

He was hired as a junior member of the foreign desk and his first big break came with the first Gulf War in 1991, after Saddam Hussein, Washington's erstwhile friend during the Iran–Iraq war, went rogue and invaded Kuwait.

Despite having spent billions on military equipment, mostly from the USA, Kuwait folded within two days and the royal family fled. President George Bush announced Operation Desert Shield, and thousands of American and other coalition troops poured into Saudi Arabia to act as a 'defensive' force. The UK provided the biggest contingent from Europe, which didn't stop American GIs referring to it as an 'itsy-bitsy army', and Miles was sent to attend the numerous press briefings, while television companies and agencies set up their satellite dishes to provide the first live front-line reporting of any war. But it was heavily censored, and most of the media were happy to go along with the authorised briefings and leave it at that. The Americans had learnt their lessons from Vietnam.

Miles found the heat unbearable. He was housed in a big tent along with other journalists and focussed on Britain's 7th armoured division, the fabled Desert Rats.

He found the press briefings boring and decided he needed to give his reports a bit of colour. To this end he spent endless hours drinking with British squaddies during their downtime, and befriended one particular tank crew. When Operation Desert Shield became Operation Desert Storm at the beginning of 1991, and the US-led coalition went on the offensive, Miles managed to get himself embedded in a Warrior tracked vehicle accompanying nearly two hundred Challenger 1 tanks.

The Iraqis put up some resistance, and there were some of the biggest tank battles the world had ever seen. The Desert Rats raced through more than 200 miles of desert and scrubland in less than four days, capturing around 300 Iraqi tanks and taking 7,000 prisoners. As the Iraqis retreated up the main highway to their own country they were continually bombed; it became known as the 'Highway of Death', and the campaign was over in less than a week.

Miles' reports were well received back in London – he had managed to provide a welcome human touch to the conflict – but the newspapers were largely eclipsed by the television pictures, which resembled a video game. There was little analysis, little focus on what it was really like on the ground, and when Miles was recalled to London at the earliest opportunity to save costs, he returned a bitterly disillusioned man. His war hadn't quite lived up to expectations, and journalism increasingly appeared less about facts and more about grabbing bigger audiences with sensationalism. As the old-timers always said, never let the facts interfere with a good story.

He was given two weeks' leave and took the long, winding and expensive train down to Cornwall to spend some time with Molly. She was waiting for him with a huge hug at St Erth station when the train finally pulled in an hour late, after being delayed by trees on the line near Redruth, and they clambered into the old Volvo for the short drive back to Lannanta.

'You're a sight for sore eyes,' she told him. 'I've been so terribly worried.'

'You needn't have been, Ma,' he told her. 'I was never in any danger. Well, not really.'

'Well, you can tell me all about it. I've got a nice cottage pie in the oven, and a bottle of wine to celebrate.'

It was March and the day was blustery, with overcast skies threatening rain. A typical Cornish day for the time of year. After the heat of the desert, Miles thought it was fantastic.

He thought the cottage pie was fantastic too, and managed two huge helpings, washed down with a perfectly reasonable merlot from the local supermarket, before sitting back with a satisfied grunt. 'You've no idea how amazing that was. Army canteen food leaves a lot to be desired.'

Molly listened intently as he went on to tell her all about his exploits: the long days of boredom interspersed with brief moments of high adrenaline, the gung-ho attitude of the American troops and the quiet professionalism of the average British squaddie, the pointless loss of life, and his disillusionment with mainstream media.

'Well, you're back now; that's all that matters,' Molly told him. 'Time for some R and R; isn't that what they call it? And I've got tickets for the Minack for Saturday night.' The Minack was a spectacular open-air theatre looking out over the North Atlantic from the cliffs near Land's End.

'What's showing?'

'*Antigone*. The reviews are very good.'

'Brilliant. I'll look forward to that. Might get some surfing in tomorrow as well, clear the old cobwebs out.'

'Oh,' Molly remembered. 'And you had a call, your chum from university, Hugh? He wants you to call him back, said it was quite important.'

'I'll do it tomorrow as well. Don't want anything to spoil this perfect evening.'

CHAPTER TWENTY

A Campaign of Letters

Annabelle held one of her 'picnics' in a park near Reading University, attired as ever in her blond wig, dark sunglasses and headscarf. She also had on a pair of light cotton gloves.

'Right, now listen up carefully,' she told the attendees. 'I'm going to give each of you a letter. They're designed to look like letter bombs, but they're not. It's just to scare people. They're all addressed to local councillors, police officers or in a couple of cases MPs. I want each of you to post one of them, but not from your local area, and make sure you wear gloves. Do not, under any circumstances, touch them with your hands, or even put them in your pocket where they can pick up fibres or whatever. Understood? They're all in sealed plastic bags and stamped, so all you have to do, once you've got your gloves on, is open the bag, post your letter, then destroy the bag, preferably by burning. Got that? We don't want any stupid mistakes.'

The dozen of her 'members' with her all nodded eagerly. At last, they were getting some action. They were a mixed bunch: a couple of students who were into right-wing politics, two women in their thirties searching for a cause after life seemed to have passed them by, and the rest middle-aged to older men angry about the way the country was heading.

Annabelle passed the sealed envelopes around. 'Best not to even look at the addresses,' she added. 'The less you know, the better for your own safety. Try to post them within the next forty-eight hours, and if any of you work out of town, the further away, the better.'

Eleven of the letters *were* fake and harmless. But one was not. Four days later the real one burst into flames as a planning officer in Sheffield opened his post, badly injuring his hands, burning his face and scorching his eyebrows.

The others were opened across the country, mystifying the recipients, who found nothing inside except a tangle of wires and a cryptic note which read, *You're on the list*. The notes were signed *The Committee of Retribution*. Most thought nothing of it, that it was just some prank, but after the Sheffield incident the police were called in, and then the anti-terrorist squad. Only five of the letters had survived; the others had been binned.

The media lost no time in screaming about 'far-right' extremism. The whole country was warned to be on the alert, and everyone was asked to snitch on their neighbours.

'Fucking result!' Vic chortled as he knocked back his favoured Scotch and water, no ice, watching the television news. 'What's next?'

'Now we lie low,' Annabelle said as she sipped her own chilled Picpoul white wine from Languedoc. 'We have all the time in the world, and we want them to think this was a one-off. That the threat has gone away.'

Vic looked at her. 'You're a genius, you know that? Have I ever told you before?'

'As a matter of fact, you have. Now come here, give us a hug. This is just the beginning.'

Just then, a telephone jangled into life, making them both jump.

'Who the fuck is that?' asked Vic, taking out his mobile.

'It's the house phone, for Christ's sake. For a start, your mobile doesn't sound anything like that with its stupid Greensleeves theme.'

'Oh, right.' Vic ambled into the hallway and picked up the landline, a number not given to many. 'Vic Jennings here.'

'It's Miles,' said the voice at the other end. 'You remember?'

'Course I do, mate. How're things? What can I do you for?'

'It's nothing urgent, just that my friend Hugh was looking for you but he's lost your number. Says he might have something for you, but I didn't want to hand out your number without asking.'

'Absolutely right. The MP, right? Well, sure, that's fine, you can give him my mobile number... this house one is for special friends only, if you know what I mean.' The line crackled. 'Where are you, anyway? Sounds a long way off, but maybe it's just a bad line.'

'I'm in Cornwall, be back in town in a week.'

'Well, be sure to give us a tinkle when you're up this way; we'll have a drink. I go up to London quite a lot these days. Business is doing well.'

'I will,' Miles assured him. 'Looking forward to it.' He rang off, and Vic replaced his receiver.

'And?' Annabelle looked at him with arched eyebrows.

'It was Miles. Seems that MP bloke, Hugh, you remember, the one we had lunch with at the Telegraph in the summer? He wants to get in touch. Says he might have something.'

'Interesting,' she said, finishing her wine and getting up for a refill. 'Want another yourself?'

CHAPTER TWENTY-ONE

AN ENTICING PROPOSAL

Hugh called Vic a couple of days later, catching him in his new Mercedes company van. On the side new livery and a fancy logo announced *V Jennings Bespoke Refurbishments & Renovations.* In smaller letters underneath it said, *No job too big or small,* with the number of his new office in Vauxhall.

'Is that you, Vic? It's Hugh, remember me? Miles gave me your number.'

'Never forget a face or a friend. How can I help?'

'Well, something has come up which I think might interest you.'

'Hang on, let me pull over.' Vic miraculously found an empty parking space in the street in Stockwell he was driving through. 'Okay, I'm listening.'

'There are three new tenders going out for maintenance in the House of Commons. Big money, guaranteed payments, long-term project. That's what you're after, isn't it?'

Vic took his pen and notepad out and started making notes. 'Sounds right up my street. So what's the deal? How do I apply?'

'Probably better if we meet up,' Hugh told him. 'Miles will be in London again after the weekend, so why don't we all get together?'

They got together in the bar of the Station Hotel at Victoria, a conveniently anonymous place of transient customers, where strangers wouldn't stand out. Outside the station, the rain teemed down.

Once they'd ordered drinks, Hugh explained the deal. Vic and Annabelle listened intently, while Miles gazed through the windows at the mass of humanity rushing to and fro, dragging suitcases and clutching mobile phones to their ears, as if the very world's existence depended upon their urgency.

'It's in several parts,' Hugh said. 'There's mechanical and electrical work to be done, some conservation stuff, and other minor restoration work. The budget is pretty big – around 300 million, I think, split between the three components – and the work is scheduled to last at least five years, maybe longer. Is that the sort of thing you're looking for?'

'Spot on,' Vic replied as Annabelle nodded her agreement. 'Although the conservation and restoration stuff are probably better suited to us. Not sure about the mechanical and electrical bit, but maybe.'

'My advice is not to bid on every project, anyway,' Hugh said. 'Just focus on one, possibly two.' He quickly outlined the application process. 'It'll all go to the Houses of Parliament Restoration and Renewal Delivery Authority for a decision.'

'Bit a mouthful,' Vic observed. 'So who's on that?'

'Some MPs, advisors, so-called experts, the usual.'

'Are you on it?'

'Maybe. We don't know the full makeup of the authority yet. But yes, it's possible.'

Vic nodded. 'Good bloody job, mate; we're indebted to you. If this comes off, I'll buy you a drink.'

'I hope that's not a euphemism.'

Annabelle laughed and raised her glass to him. 'Our thanks. We won't forget this.'

Miles stood and stretched. 'Well, I don't know about the rest of you, but I need to get back to the office. And it's really stuffy in here. Need to get some fresh air, though God knows where I'll find that in this city.'

Vic slapped him on the back. 'That night I saved your arse in Reading could prove to be the luckiest day of my life. We'll catch up soon. You need to come and see our new office in Vauxhall; you'll like it.'

CHAPTER TWENTY-TWO

Genocide in Africa

Aboard a Hercules cargo plane carrying relief supplies, Miles gazed with wonder and some trepidation at the thick jungle and undulating hills below.

A week earlier, on 7th April 1994, after the assassination of the Rwandan president Juvénal Habyarimana, the Rwandan Hutu army and assorted armed groups had started to massacre their Tutsi rivals in their thousands. The world looked on and expressed shock, but did nothing. Miles was by now an assistant foreign editor, and had quickly volunteered for the assignment, while others demurred.

'It's Africa,' one old hand had advised him. 'It's totally unpredictable. When they run amok anything can happen; they're fucking savages, drugged to the eyeballs.'

Molly was also horrified at the idea of Miles going there and tried to change his mind, but finally accepted the inevitable.

'It's what I do, Ma. Don't worry, I'll be careful; I'll be fine,' he reassured her. 'See you in a few weeks.'

The plane landed in the Rwandan capital, Kigali. After a rigorous search of his luggage, during which he lost the carton of 200 Marlboros he'd packed for that very purpose, Miles was waved through by sullen troops toting AK-47s. He was given a cot in a United Nations compound along with an assortment of other journalists from around the world: Brits from the television agencies Visnews and UPITN, a smattering of French and Americans, and even a couple of Japanese.

For the next few days, the assorted journalists were confined to reporting on airlifts coming in and out of Kigali airport, drinking beer and swapping past war stories of derring-do. Going anywhere alone was too dangerous. Already ten Belgian soldiers with the United Nations Assistance Mission in Rwanda, or UNAMIR, had been captured at the national radio station and taken to the Camp Kigali military base, where they were tortured and killed. There was also a standoff at the national parliament building, which was occupied by Tutsi troops of the Rwandan Patriotic Front, RPF, who had repulsed an attack by government soldiers. But Miles was at least pleasantly surprised by the temperature; instead of being insufferably hot as he'd expected, the climate was temperate, thanks to the altitude.

A week later, Miles was allowed to join a UN relief column heading towards a supposed refugee camp near the border with Zaire. He shared space in a Land Cruiser with a cameraman from UPITN - a jovial shaven-headed Romanian called Olimpiu who he instinctively liked - and a reporter from the French wire agency AFP. They drove, throwing up a cloud of dust, along a road littered with bodies by the side: men, women and children, with scavengers picking through the dead in search of anything of value.

Before the border they came across the rear of a horde of refugees, desperate to cross into Zaire; in their midst Rwandan soldiers and militia were shooting indiscriminately and hacking at people with machetes and clubs. It was a scene from hell. They stopped at a checkpoint.

'Where's the goddam refugee camp?' a Belgian UN soldier demanded of the soldiers.

'No refugee camp,' a captain with red eyes replied. 'You go back, nothing to see here.'

'This is outrageous! We have humanitarian aid!'

'Give your aid to me; we will distribute it,' the soldier ordered, threatening them with his rifle.

The thirty other Belgian troops with the convoy immediately took up defensive positions and pointed their own weapons. For what seemed like an eternity, no one moved. Miles lay flat in the Land Cruiser, and was astonished when Olimpiu got out of the car, holding his camera in one hand by his side, a piece of gaffer tape stuck over the telltale blinking red light which would show he was recording.

Finally, the Hutu officer shrugged and lowered his rifle. 'No refugees; you go back.' He turned away, more intent on the genocide than getting into a firefight.

There was no choice. They turned around to go back to Kigali.

'Shit, man, what's going on?' Miles was despondent.

'They're killing everyone,' Olimpiu replied, jovial no more.

'You were filming, taking a big fucking risk. Did you get anything?'

'I hope so. If you don't put the camera to your eye, mostly they don't realise what you're doing.' Olimpiu rewound his tape and played it back. 'Yes, I got it all. At least we have a story.'

Miles was amazed. He'd not come across agency people before, and they were a breed apart, the unsung heroes of the news business. When he filed his story that evening, he gave full credit to Olimpiu's bravery, and the story made the front page.

In response to the UN's pleas, the RPF commander in the north of the country, Paul Kagame, had refused to negotiate a ceasefire unless the killing stopped. It didn't, and the seasoned troops of the RPF had gone on the offensive. They quickly made gains against the undisciplined government soldiers and soon liberated swathes of the country in the north and east, putting an end to the genocide in those areas. By the end of the month, they had secured the entire Tanzanian border area and began their push on Kigali, desperate to relieve their isolated comrades in the capital.

The RPF cut the road from Kigali to Gitarama, which had become the temporary home of the Hutu government, at the end of May. Miles set off with Olimpiu, along with two reporters from the *Washington Post* and *Frankfurter Allgemeine* newspapers, in a posse of armour-plated four-wheel-drive vehicles, paying several South African and German mercenaries to act as protection.

'This is insane,' Miles shouted, pumped up with adrenaline, as they sped up the main road out of Kigali. 'What if we get stopped?

What if the RPF don't play ball?'

'We don't stop. And trust me, the RPF will be fine. They're very disciplined; I was in their camps in Uganda once. They want friends,' Olimpiu assured him, patting his shoulder. He was wearing a cameraman's jacket with pockets everywhere and carried a shoulder bag stuffed with spare cassettes.

Olimpiu was right. When they came to the first RPF checkpoint they were treated cautiously but politely. One of the mercs who spoke Kinyarwanda, the main language of all ethnic groups in Rwanda, explained who they were, that they meant no harm and that they wanted to help the RPF cause.

After everyone was searched, and the mercs were relieved of their weapons on the promise that they would be returned in good time, they were ordered to follow a young sergeant with a group of six other soldiers. They didn't have far to go before reaching a clearing with a large command tent, and there was Paul Kagame himself, standing over six feet and dressed in military fatigues, bespectacled and very thin, with bony shoulders. He welcomed them graciously, and offered them tea and cold mizuzu: fried plantains.

He agreed to an interview, which Olimpiu was allowed to film, and told them they could accompany his army to Kigali. 'The war is nearly over,' he said. 'We will be in the capital before the end of June; this I promise you.'

It was an optimistic prediction, but only just. The victorious RPF soldiers entered and seized Kigali on the 4th of July, with Miles, Olimpiu and the other two reporters in tow. During the advance, Miles had been allowed to send his dispatches by satellite phone, while Olimpiu sent his tapes back with the mercs to a colleague in the capital, whence they were flown back to Europe. Both of them enjoyed exclusives that left the competition seething.

The killing had gone on for a hundred days, in which more than half a million Tutsis were estimated to have died, by gun, machete or crude clubs, while another quarter of a million women were raped, many of them subsequently succumbing to HIV. And still the world had done nothing.

CHAPTER TWENTY-THREE

A New Player Appears

Back in Westminster, Hugh had lost his position as a junior minister in the Home Office and was on the back benches. He was viewed as a Thatcherite and had ardently opposed the Maastricht Treaty, neither of which had endeared him to the wets who now made up the inner circle of John Major's government. But he was a pragmatic person and happy to lie low, well aware that everything went in cycles and sure that his time would come around again.

In the meantime, he devoted himself to constituency work and to getting himself onto as many minor committees as possible, including the all-important Houses of Parliament Restoration and Renewal Delivery Authority. It hadn't been difficult as there wasn't exactly a queue to join the body, but Hugh had a gut feeling about Miles' strange friend Vic and his alluring girlfriend. He thought Vic was something of a rough diamond, but also felt their futures were somehow inextricably linked.

On the other side of the House of Commons, Tony Blair had just been elected leader of the opposition Labour Party, something that made Hugh uneasy. Blair was too smarmy by half. Like most politicians, he never answered a direct question, but it wasn't just that. His eyes were weird, kind of manic, he was an ideologue who didn't read books and had no knowledge of history, and he was too smooth. One day he was Scottish, the next a Newcastle United supporter: one of those 'all things to all men' people, which everyone knew was the sign of a true snake oil salesman. A 'man of the people' was how he portrayed himself, although he was anything but; he cared for no one but himself and his bank balance. But Hugh was well aware of how seductive his message was, and how gullible people were. And all there was standing between him and number 10 Downing Street was John Major.

'Blair's going to be trouble, I reckon,' Hugh told a fellow MP as he drank deeply from his subsidised gin and tonic in a House of Commons bar.

'You think?' replied the other, a rotund man with florid cheeks and cheap suit who was drinking a large brandy to wash down his own substantial subsidised lunch.

'Even if he just seems a bad egg all round, we're playing into his hands. Black Wednesday, getting kicked out of the ERM – thank God of course, but people don't see that – Maastricht, inflation through the roof, plus the left still hate Maggie and blame her for all our ills. So yes, I think we need to prepare for the worst,' Hugh said bluntly.

'I got one of those letters, you know, just the other day,' his companion said, apropos of nothing.

'What letters?'

'You know, the ones that have been posted to public figures all over the country. My secretary opened it, but thankfully it was just a jumble of wires, a fake. Told the police, of course, but I suppose nothing will come of it.'

'Blimey.'

*

In Scotland Yard, Detective Inspector James Parker was at his wits' end.

'Another eight of these letters that we know of,' he addressed his team, using a pointer to show where each had been reported on a map of the country. They were north, south, east and west. 'Only one was the real thing, addressed to one of our own in Hampshire, no less, but fortunately a postal worker in a sorting office got suspicious and reported it.' He reached for his cigarettes, then remembered smoking had been banned in the office and put the packet back in his pocket. The room stank of stale sweat and cheap takeaway food.

'Fingerprints, guv?' asked a slovenly-looking man with long lank hair at the back of the group. He was wearing a bomber jacket and jeans. One of the undercover guys.

'Nothing. Not a hint, not even any fibres. The only thing that links them is that they've clearly all been written on the same typewriter. If we can trace that, then we can crack this.'

'How are we supposed to do that?' asked a pretty WPC who was on attachment to the detective unit.

'I understand all typewriters have a signature of some sort. Could be a faulty key, the typeface itself, whatever. We need to at least try and narrow it down to a make. Find a typewriter expert, for a start. Come on, let's get to work!' He tried unsuccessfully to instil some enthusiasm.

The group dispersed mumbling, unhappy at the impossibility of their task. Some headed to the coffee machine, some to their desks, and a couple downstairs for a fag break.

CHAPTER TWENTY-FOUR

The Surprise Baby

Annabelle was as surprised as anyone when she discovered she was pregnant. When she was first sick in the morning, she thought it must have been something she ate. But when it happened a second and a third time, she started to put two and two together.

She tested herself, then retested and retested again, and still the result was positive. She thought she'd been so careful, and neither she nor Vic had ever expressed any desire to have children. It didn't fit with their plans. But she didn't like the idea of a termination. In fact, it repelled her. She stood in the bathroom and stroked her naked stomach, and wondered how Vic would react.

She waited until after the evening dinner. She had cooked him one of his favourites, rib-eye steak, medium rare – he liked it red in the middle but not with the blood running out – with fries and a side salad, accompanied by a decent vintage of Saint-Émilion wine. She also ate heartily, even if her steak was smaller, and watched him polish off his food as they made small talk.

'Fantastic, absolutely bloody brilliant,' Vic said as he finally put his knife and fork down. He leaned back with a sigh.

'Yeah, well, special dinner, 'cause I've got something special to tell you.' Annabelle took a sip of her wine.

'You do? Okay, I'm all ears; surprise me!'

'You sure you want to hear this?'

'Well, I won't fucking know till you tell me, love, will I? Come on, the suspense is killing me!'

'And then there were three.'

Vic paused with his glass halfway to his mouth. Outside it was a brilliant spring day; the French doors to the garden were open, the bluebells were out and the jasmine flowering. 'Eh? What does that mean? Is this some kind of cryptic quiz?'

'Oh, come on, Vic! I'm pregnant!'

'You're *what*? Preg...' The word trailed off, then his face lit up with a goofy grin, and he stood up. 'Bloody hell, Bella, come here, let me give you a squeeze. That's just amazing! How did we do that?' And he wrapped his arms around her.

Tears glistened in her eyes. Whatever she had expected, it wasn't this. 'How do you think, you daft bugger? I dunno, maybe I missed a day or two. I thought I was being careful. I'm sorry.'

'Sorry?' he exclaimed. 'Sorry? Well, I'm bloody not. I think this is the best news ever, and I mean ever! Come on, we need to celebrate, a glass of shampoo at the least!' He paused. 'And you? Are you happy?'

'Oh, yes, Vic. At first I wasn't sure, but then I knew I couldn't get rid of it. It's something we've made together, you and me, and I was so worried about what you'd think.'

'I love you, Bella, and I couldn't be happier! We'll have a beautiful baby, and you'll be a beautiful mother. Now, about that champagne...'

'Okay, then. Just a glass for me; I shouldn't be drinking so much now, you know.'

'Got to wet the baby's head, you know,' Vic told her. 'So I'll just have to drink for three.'

Annabelle laughed. 'Wetting the baby's head is supposed to be after it's born! And when did you ever not drink for three?'

*

Miles paid a visit after his latest post-war break in Cornwall, stopping off in Reading on his way back to London. He was looking suntanned and exuding good health after two weeks of home cooking and time on the surfboard.

'We want you to be the godfather, mate,' Vic said, once they'd broken the news to him. They'd become good friends, and Vic didn't have many.

'My honour; I'm so happy for you!' Miles told them, and Annabelle beamed at him, looking radiant in a loose-fitting pearl grey silk dress. They were sitting out on the patio, a pitcher of Pimm's full of fruit on the table and a cool breeze from the river alleviating the heat of the afternoon.

'I used to work over there, remember?' Miles pointed across the river to where the offices of the *Evening Post* lay partially hidden by trees.

'And now look at you,' Annabelle replied. 'Top gun. So, tell us about your latest exploits.'

'First things first. The big news is that I've got a girl. I mean a serious one; I think she might be the one, if you know what I mean.'

'Oh, I know, mate; I know all right. That's top news,' Vic assured him, holding up his glass for a clink. 'Cheers!'

Annabelle clapped her hands. 'That's wonderful, Miles. What's her name? When do we get to meet her?'

'She's called Delen. It's a Celtic name, Cornish Celtic; it means "petal". She's a nurse from Camborne, old tin mining town not far from my own home, although she's working in London at the moment. We met at a party a couple of months ago, and just seemed to click. Maybe it helps that we're both from Cornwall and can't stand London. In fact, we're thinking we might go back to the West Country one of these days, try something different.'

'Amazing, well done you!' Annabelle said. 'Well, I can't wait to meet her.'

'I've always fancied a holiday home in Cornwall,' Vic said, and they laughed.

Miles went on to tell them all about Rwanda, how fucked up it all was. 'And while I was there, seems South Africa held their first elections with universal suffrage. The ANC won, of course, and Mandela is president. Twenty-seven years in prison, and now he's the president; how's that for a turnaround?'

Vic shrugged. 'Well, they'll fuck that place up as well. Just like whatshisface in Rhodesia, just watch.'

'It's Zimbabwe now, do keep up,' Miles jokingly admonished him.

'Whatever, I tell you South Africa will go the same way. Your average darkie couldn't run a bath, let alone a country.'

'That's a bit harsh, isn't it? I mean, apartheid was just wrong; anyone can see that. It was only a matter of time before we saw black majority rule.'

'That may be.' Vic looked at him. 'But mark my words, it'll all end in tears, and somehow we'll get the blame. Rainbow fucking nation, my arse. I read a book about Rhodesia; it was called *Don't Let's Go to the Dogs Tonight*, I think that was it, told you all you need to know. And anyway, I wouldn't mind a bit of apartheid here, to be honest; bastards are taking over.'

'Now you're being paranoid.' Miles helped himself to another glass of Pimm's. 'We all share the same world; we need to get on with each other. It's the way it's going, and you can't turn back the tide; you're not King Canute.'

'Actually, that story is also rubbish,' Annabelle informed him. 'He wasn't trying to turn back the tide. In fact, he was proving to his adoring hangers-on that kings are not infallible. That they're just humans. Didn't you know that?'

'I didn't, as a matter of fact,' Miles conceded. 'That's interesting.'

'How many darkies in Cornwall?' Vic asked.

'Not many,' Miles admitted.

'Well enough of world politics,' Vic announced, standing up. 'Time to fire up the barbecue.'

As it happened, although he didn't know it at the time, Vic's predictions were prescient. It took about thirty years, but in that time endemic corruption and mismanagement wrecked South Africa's economy. Instead of the country being an economic shining beam of hope for the continent, the roads had potholes the size of bomb craters and the country was suffering under rolling blackouts, crime was through the roof, and black South Africans fought pitched battles with migrants from Zimbabwe, Nigeria and the Congo in Johannesburg's Hill Brow suburb, claiming they were stealing their jobs.

CHAPTER TWENTY-FIVE

A Bibendum Dinner

Hugh watched on with dismay as Tony Blair won a landslide victory at the general election in 1997, ending eighteen years of Tory rule. Hugh himself kept his seat, his focus on constituency work since falling down in the Tory pecking order paying dividends.

'He's pure bloody evil in my view, a warmonger. I mean, just what exactly are we doing sticking our nose into Kosovo? Bunch of bloody Albanians move across the border and start settling there, and then claim it as their own! It's like the Pakistanis claiming Bradford as an independent state. Kosovo belongs to Serbia, pure and simple; they were our friends in World War Two, and now we're backing the Muslims! The Albanians have got their own country; it's called Albania!' Hugh was rarely this angry.

'Calm down. You're not on the campaign trail now; we're supposed to be celebrating.' Miles put a hand on Hugh's arm.

They were together with Vic, Annabelle and Delen, dining at the Bibendum seafood restaurant in South Kensington, and the oysters had just arrived in a large silver platter on a bed of ice. The table was wide and circular, the chairs comfortable, and the tablecloth and proper napkins starched and crisp in the old style. Hugh had suggested a brasserie in St James's instead, but Vic had said it was too noisy and full of posh wankers, and as he was paying his preference won the day. South Kensington was also closer to the small flat Vic and Annabelle had bought in Chelsea as a London base for part of the week, and convenient too for the place Miles and Delen had bought together in Clapham Common.

Miles turned to Annabelle. 'So, how's the princess Alice? What is she, two years old now?'

'Yes, just over two, and in wonderland.' She smiled back at him. 'At least I hope so, with the babysitter anyway, and she was fast asleep when we left.'

Annabelle had actually enjoyed her pregnancy, against all expectations. Despite the discomfort of the last couple of months, when she had swollen like a balloon and it was impossible to sit, sleep or walk comfortably, her overriding feeling was one of pride. Pride at bringing a living being into the world, one that she instinctively knew would be beautiful and kind.

She had been lucky enough to have an easy birth; despite the pain, it was over within a couple of hours of going into labour. Their daughter was nothing if not beautiful, with a head of thick hair which astonished the midwives, and Annabelle's dark penetrating eyes. Vic had astonished himself by bursting into tears.

Now they were celebrating because Vic had indeed won one of the contracts for the House of Commons maintenance, in no small thanks to Hugh's role on the Restoration and Renewal Authority. Vic had secured the job of repairing the basements of the Commons and making them safe.

'So, you're going to be a millionaire?' Delen teased him with a sly smile. She was a small girl, a couple of inches shorter than Miles, but with strong features: an aquiline nose, prominent cheekbones and, like many Cornish, a slightly dusky skin colour compared to most English people, as if she had a permanent suntan. Her shoulder-length hair was jet black, and her eyes were a startling green. She was wearing a smart navy-blue trouser suit with white piping, and sipped at her glass of cold champagne.

'More of one, my dear, more of one; the world's our oyster now. Talking of which, do tuck in.' He nodded at the platter on the table.

As they helped themselves to the oysters, Vic turned to Hugh. 'And what about your woman?'

'Sophie? We parted, or rather she ditched me when we lost the election. Think she was hoping I'd be a minister, so she's gone hunting for better prospects, I suspect.' Hugh, dressed in casual linen trousers and a crumpled pale yellow linen shirt, was no longer as thin as in his student days. He wasn't fat, but his chest had filled out somewhat, and he was developing a distinct paunch thanks to his multiple subsidised lunches and drinks.

'You're well out of it if you ask me, mate,' Vic said. 'You know, I used to think you were a stuck-up rich twat, but you're okay for a politician.'

'Thanks for the compliment,' Hugh said, smiling. He squeezed some lemon onto the oyster he was holding and added a dash of tabasco. 'But my family aren't actually that rich. They're farmers. It's true we own a few hundred acres, mostly given over to sheep and some arable, but it's hard work and the margins are thin. One bad summer can wipe out a whole year's profits.'

Vic nodded. 'Yeah, I guess the big money these days seems to be with all the spivs in the city. Maybe I missed a trick there, but I like doing what I do, and it's solid; it's something I can touch and feel, not like all that fake money.'

'Anyway, going back to Sophie, you're right; I'm well rid of her. It wasn't working out anyway, and someone else will come along,' Hugh assured him philosophically. 'Women are like buses: none in sight for ages, and then half a dozen turn up at the same time. And I'm not in a hurry, although I do have to say I'm jealous of you lot.'

They waited while the waiters cleared away the debris of their oysters and served the main course: pan-fried Dover sole for Hugh and Miles, grilled sea bass for Delen, poached salmon for Annabelle and an enormous oven-baked turbot for Vic. A couple of bottles of Annabelle's favourite Pouilly-Fumé white wine accompanied the food.

'What about you, Miles?' Annabelle asked. She was wearing a bright red dress, her hair tied back in a ponytail. 'You said you were thinking of going back to Cornwall?'

'*We're* thinking about it,' he corrected her. 'Yes, eventually. Might take another couple of years, we need to save up, but yes, we want to go back. Cornwall is a beautiful part of the country, the air is cleaner, and the water is soft, not like the hard chalky stuff you get in London. People might be poorer than London, but it's just a better way of life, no stress or aggression. And not really any crime, outside the tourist season, anyway. And we both want to be near family.'

'But what will you do there? Won't you miss the cut and thrust of the city?' Hugh pitched in.

'We won't miss London at all. When I'm down in Cornwall I don't even watch the TV news; your Westminster bubble means nothing to most people down there. As for what we'll do, well, Delen can work as a nurse if need be, at least to begin with. I've got my heart set on a surfing school, but I'm not sure if that would generate enough money to see us through the winter. Either that or a cider farm.'

'Good for you, sounds idyllic,' Vic said. 'Don't think it'd suit me, I think I need the buzz of the city, but then I'm just a bundle of nervous energy anyway. Ask Bella. I'd go mad sitting on a beach all day. You better get a big place, though, because we'll be coming to visit.'

'I hope you'll be coming in October,' Delen said, holding up her left hand, on which a small diamond ring twinkled. 'We're getting married.'

'No way!' Annabelle put her napkin to her mouth. 'I saw the ring but didn't want to say anything. Was wondering when you might own up. Tell us, come on.'

'It'll be in my local church in Lannanta,' Miles informed her. 'My dad's buried in the churchyard there, overlooking the estuary. Then we'll have the reception in the Beach Club Restaurant, right by the beach in Porthreptor. That's Carbis Bay to you.'

'Why do you have to keep changing all the names down there?' Annabelle asked.

Miles shrugged. 'We didn't change them; the English did, and I guess some of us just want to hold on to the old culture and language. It's a bit like Wales; all the signs are in two languages.'

'Fair enough. Well, can't wait to get the invitations; we'll be there for sure.'

'You better. Hugh is going to be best man, and Vic the chief usher.'

'I am?' Hugh said with surprise.

'What's an usher do?' asked Vic.

'Top hat and tails, mate – hire them at Moss Bros if you need to – and it's your job to usher people to their seats in the church. We're going all traditional. And you'll stay in the Carbis Bay Hotel, guests of honour; you'll love it. Bring your swimming gear as well.'

'I need to get a new dress!' Annabelle said.

CHAPTER TWENTY-SIX

THE WORLD CHANGES

Hugh's misgivings about Tony Blair were confirmed as the New Labour Prime Minister presided over a massive increase in public spending, reversing many of Thatcher's savings for the taxpayer, while expanding rights for the LGBT community, banning fox hunting and granting devolution to Scotland and Wales. Even though he was a politician himself, Hugh couldn't for the life of him see why such a small island needed three parliaments – plus another in Northern Ireland – along with all the useless non-productive hangers-on that members of the various parliaments brought in their wake. Politicians seemed to be the biggest growth industry in the country.

And then the world changed on a Tuesday afternoon, or morning in the United States, on 11th September 2001, when a Boeing 767 airliner packed with passengers slammed into the north tower of the World Trade Centre in New York.

'Miles, turn on your TV!' Hugh yelled down the telephone.

Miles was sitting in his new home in Carbis Bay, a detached two-storey stone cottage above the main St Ives Road. He and Delen had just returned from the West Cornwall Hospital in Penzance with their newborn son, named Piran after the patron saint of the county, who had been delivered by Caesarean section after turning in the womb three days earlier. Piran was asleep in his cot.

'Hang on, mate, we've just got back from the hospital, about to have a glass of champagne.'

'Just turn it on. Now!'

With some annoyance, Miles picked up the remote control and pushed the 'on' button, just in time to see the second airliner smash into the south tower seventeen minutes after the first.

'For fuck's sake,' he muttered. 'What's going on?' He called out to Delen and Molly, who were in the kitchen.

'You watching?' Hugh shouted.

'Yeah, yeah, I'm watching. Oh my God.'

'I'll call you later,' Hugh said, and rang off.

For the rest of the afternoon, Miles, Delen and Molly watched spellbound, drinking their champagne as first the south tower and then the north tower collapsed in a mass of smoke and debris. Desperate people could be seen jumping from the upper floors of the north tower, their escape routes via the stairs cut off by the fires and smoke. News came in of another aeroplane crashing into the Pentagon, while a fourth aircraft crashed into the Pennsylvania countryside after the passengers tried to overcome the hijackers.

'Oh, Lordy, Lordy, the Yanks aren't going to like that,' Miles said.

'It's too awful,' Molly said. 'Who would do such a thing?'

'Al-Qaeda, Osama bin Laden. America is going to go absolutely nuts.'

'Some world we've brought Piran into,' Delen commented, as she got ready to give him a feed.

'Makes you glad to be here in Cornwall, not back up in London,' Miles said. 'There'll be all sorts of shit going on now.'

*

Almost three thousand people died in the 11th September attacks, which the Americans were soon calling 9/11, because they always get the day of the month and month itself the wrong way around. Most of the victims were in the twin towers, along with firefighters and rescue workers, while more than a hundred died at the Pentagon, and the rest were killed in the fourth airliner when it crashed. It could have been worse, as it was estimated there were up to eight thousand people in each of the twin towers, but Miles was right; America was like a hornet's nest that had been dropped on the ground.

According to Hugh, who'd been speaking with one of his

opposite numbers in the Labour Party in the aftermath, Tony Blair had heard the news while sitting in the Grand Hotel in Brighton, where he was preparing to address the Trades Union Congress. Word had it that he had immediately decided to back the United States to the hilt, supporting whatever course of action they took, enthusiastically egged on by his manic and allegedly alcoholic spin doctor, Alistair Campbell. The next month they began bombing Afghanistan, leading to one of the longest wars in modern history.

But Afghanistan was just the precursor to the Second Gulf War, and the invasion of Iraq.

'The guy's insane!' Hugh was on the telephone to Miles again. 'It doesn't seem that long ago that Saddam was our best mate when he was slugging it out with Iran. Rumsfeld was practically kneeling at his feet! Now they seem determined to take him out.'

'All seems a long way from here,' Miles told him. 'But it does seem extreme. Can't see what it's got to do with us.'

Miles and Delen had forged a new life since moving back to Cornwall. They'd been lucky with the house, getting into the market just before prices took off in the Carbis Bay area, and were astonished by how much they'd made on the flat in Clapham Common. They'd been able to put down a hefty deposit on the three-bedroom cottage, which cost them less than a one-bedroom flat in a nice part of the capital. It had a wood-burning stove in the beamed lounge to back up the central heating, a black Aga range cooker dominating the kitchen with its red tiled floor, and a decent but manageable garden where they were growing a variety of fruits and vegetables.

True to his word, Miles had won the concession to run the sea sports centre in Carbis Bay and could now walk to work, renting out surfboards, canoes, small sailing boats and paddleboards from Easter through to the end of October, while in the winter he carried out local odd jobs, cleaning gutters, fixing fences or whatever was needed.

He also gave surfing and sailing lessons, and there was plenty of demand, especially at the height of the tourist season, when families descended in droves from all over the country and Europe. It was easy to see why. The fine sandy beaches were as good as anywhere in the world in his view; the water was translucent, if a bit cool – but nothing that a wetsuit couldn't sort out – and the light ethereal, a major attraction for artists. The sea in Carbis Bay was also safe. It was an enclosed bay facing northeast and there was hardly any current, unlike the next few beaches further up the coast, facing west, which were ridden with riptides and strong undercurrents. The days were long, but he couldn't imagine anything better, and he was happy.

Delen, meanwhile, worked two days a week in a care home, when Molly took over babysitting duties, and otherwise helped out at the beach when time allowed.

Their joint annual income was less than half what it had been in London, but their outgoings were much lower too – not quite half, but not far off – and the quality of life bore no comparison to the city. They could walk to just about anywhere they needed: a supermarket ten minutes away, a bakery, dentist, hairdresser's and opticians. Even St Ives, with its array of restaurants and the Tate Modern, could be reached on foot within half an hour on the coastal path. They both felt that they'd made the right decision.

'Don't you miss it?' Hugh asked. 'London, I mean. You could be on your way back to the desert; I'm sure there's going to be another war.'

Miles laughed. 'I miss it like I'd miss a boil on my arse, mate. No way would I want to go back to all that. We're living in paradise down here. Take a break, come and visit us.'

'I will when I can; maybe a long weekend in the autumn? That's assuming we're not all in a bunker somewhere. Promise.'

*

In September 2002 Blair presented his 'dodgy dossier' to the House of Commons, claiming that Iraq had weapons of mass destruction that could be activated within forty-five minutes: another document that had the fingerprints of his spin doctor, Alistair Campbell, all over it. Blair had no solid evidence, and it wasn't true, but it was enough for parliament to support going to war. Nearly two million people marched in London to oppose the invasion, but the egotistical Blair dismissed the protest out of hand.

The vote to support the invasion was passed in parliament in March 2003 by 412 to 149. 254 Labour MPs were among those who enthusiastically backed the war, along with 149 Tories. Hugh decided he had food poisoning that day and didn't attend. Only two Conservatives voted against the motion; it was becoming hard to tell the difference between the two main parties in Britain.

Two days later, the American-led coalition invaded Iraq. It was a predictably one-sided affair, the Americans deploying their 'shock and awe' bombing tactics, the Iraqis retreating in disorder. Some of the toughest resistance was put up by irregular 'fedayeen' militia, which would become a sign of things to come. Baghdad had fallen by the middle of April, and Blair went on to bask in his glory as he addressed the US Congress in July and received a standing ovation.

In the event, the 'victory' in Iraq was short-lived. The country descended into chaos, and the occupiers faced a massive insurgency and daily attacks from a variety of groups, most of them at loggerheads with each other as well as the occupying coalition troops, thousands of whom died in vain. Not even the execution of Saddam Hussein in 2006 could stem the uprising, and the war dragged on until 2011.

Blair had become bored with Iraq long before then, however, and had turned his attention to literally changing the face of Britain when, in 2004, he decided to allow citizens from eight new Eastern European members of the European Community immediate rights to relocate and settle in the UK. And millions did, adding to the huge numbers already arriving from Bangladesh, India and Pakistan in particular. Germany and France were more cautious, setting limits on how many of the 'new Europeans' could cross into their countries with full rights, but Blair decided mass immigration was what Britain needed, and that's what it got.

'Diversity is our strength,' the nation was told, and it would 'enrich' everyone. Many had their doubts about this confirmed on the day after London was awarded the 2012 Olympics when, on 7th July 2005, three Islamist terrorists detonated homemade bombs on separate underground trains in the city, while a fourth detonated a bomb on a double-decker bus in Tavistock Square. More than fifty people were killed and more than seven hundred injured. It was to be the first of many such terror attacks in the years to come.

The final years of Blair's time in office saw a collapse in social cohesion, along with a steep rise in violent crime and drug dealing. He had eroded trust in British politics and become one of the most reviled people in the country, something even he could not ignore, and in mid-2007 he finally bowed to the inevitable and handed over the keys of Downing Street to his wall-eyed Scottish chancellor, Gordon Brown.

But Blair had achieved his aim of amassing a fortune for himself, and, bizarrely for what many people saw as a warmonger, he was then appointed as a special peace envoy for the Middle East and set up his own 'Tony Blair Institute for Global Change'. Those accused of being conspiracy theorists for voicing concerns about a cabal of very powerful people wanting to introduce a new global order, which would serve the interests of that same cabal, were seeing their worst fears being realised.

Years later, when Blair was awarded a knighthood by the dying Queen Elizabeth II, more than 700,000 people signed a petition opposing the award, and were ignored.

CHAPTER TWENTY-SEVEN

A Mess in the Basement

'Bloody hell,' Vic muttered as he shone his torch around, and a rat scuttled past his feet. 'The state of that!'

He was in the basement of Westminster, below the central lobby of the Houses of Parliament. Miles of high-voltage cables ran in all directions, some held together with gaffer tape. Leaking pipes dripped water into buckets and empty tins on the floor, next to overflowing rubbish bins and discarded chairs and desks. There were bits of scaffolding holding some of the leaking pipes in place and thousands of smaller wires everywhere serving God knew what purpose, which wouldn't have looked out of place above a street in Delhi or Karachi. Asbestos lined some of the walls. Despite the efforts of a few extractor fans, it was incredibly hot, and Vic was perspiring.

'You wouldn't believe it,' he told Annabelle as they sat in the garden that Friday evening, nursing their pre-dinner drinks. The weather was perfect, the sky cloudless with just the hint of a breeze. If anything, it was almost too hot for Vic, whose pale skin wasn't ideally suited to the sun. 'The whole fucking place could go up like a bomb at any time. Water and electricity aren't a good mix at the best of times.'

'Sounds promising,' Annabelle said, swirling her gin and tonic so the ice rattled in the glass, and looking at Alice.

Alice was playing on the grass, making daisy chains and singing softly to herself. She was growing into a real beauty, long-limbed and with her mother's penetrating gaze, but with a gentler personality.

She was smart too, and had won a place at Kendrick Grammar

School in Reading, one of the best girls' state schools in the country. Vic was delighted. Although they could afford it, he hadn't wanted his daughter to go to a private school where, as he put it, she would be ruined by mixing with out-of-touch rich toffs, but nor had he wanted her to go to one of the state comprehensives, which mostly catered to the lowest common denominator and churned out semi-educated louts by the thousands.

'How about we take the boat out tomorrow if the weather stays like this?' Vic suggested. 'We could go up to Henley and Sonning and have a pub lunch or a picnic, or maybe just to Mapledurham and back. What do you think?'

'Sounds ideal.' Annabelle looked back him. 'But tell me more about Westminster.'

'Not a lot to tell, really.' Vic shrugged, adjusting his straw hat to keep the sun out of his good eye. 'It's a fucking mess. It looks like they've done no proper maintenance since the place was built. I wonder if those arseholes blathering away in the chamber above have any idea of what they're sitting on. Anyway, it should keep me in a job for many years to come, so cheers to that.'

'To me, it sounds like an opportunity. Not today, not tomorrow, but something to bear in mind.' Annabelle leaned forwards and touched his knee.

'You're not suggesting...?'

'That's exactly what I'm suggesting. It's just an idea, mind; something to keep up our sleeve in case the need arises.'

'Blimey, I never thought of that, but you've got a point. What a show that would be!'

Annabelle stood up. 'It certainly would. Like they say, Guy Fawkes was the only man who entered the Houses of Parliament with honest intentions. You could be the second. Anyway, I'll get dinner; salad and garlic bread okay for you? Or do you want something more substantial?'

'Salad is fine; plenty of anchovies for me, please, and a Caesar or blue cheese dressing. Guy Fawkes, eh?' He chuckled. 'You know I signed the Official Secrets Act?'

'So what? It's just a piece of paper at the end of the day. Be back soon, we'll eat outside,' and she ducked into the house, heading for the kitchen.

CHAPTER TWENTY-EIGHT

Hugh Finally Falls in Love

Hugh looked on with no small amount of schadenfreude as Gordon Brown took a wrecking ball to the UK economy.

Having already initiated the sell-off of over half the country's gold reserves as chancellor, in one of the worst investment decisions of all time, when the price of the metal was at the bottom of a two-decades-old bear market, in 2008 he was knocked for six by the global financial crisis, triggered by the collapse of the US housing market and subprime mortgage lending.

The crisis threatened to destroy the international financial system as numerous investment and commercial banks collapsed, among them Lehman Brothers, which was the biggest bankruptcy in US history at the time. Mortgage lenders, insurance companies and savings associations all went to the wall.

In the UK, the national debt shot up as Brown used taxpayers' money to bail out the banks. The subsequent recession saw Labour's popularity plummet in the polls.

The same year saw the Lisbon Treaty signed off with no referendum, which many regarded as a betrayal of the UK's sovereignty. Only one country, Ireland, held a referendum and voted against the treaty. That was ignored, and the Irish were told to go away and vote again until they got the 'right' result. The Czechs and Poles also had severe reservations but finally passed the treaty under extreme pressure. It allowed for the end of the EC's economic framework, with all its powers and structures to be incorporated into the EU, and the office of a permanent EU president was created. It was the birth of a federal Europe led by unelected commissioners, the very antithesis of democracy.

The final nail in Brown's coffin came as he was campaigning for the 2010 election in Rochdale, part of the Greater Manchester urban sprawl in Lancashire. Brown was busy pressing the flesh, trying to achieve the impossible of appearing as a man of the people, when he was confronted by a pensioner, Gillian Duffy, about the problems of the overwhelmed public services and mass immigration.

'All these Eastern Europeans what are coming in, where are they all flocking from?' asked Gillian.

Being Scottish, Brown may have misunderstood her thick Lancashire accent; maybe he thought she said 'fucking' instead of 'flocking'. Either way, he seemed irritated and told her, 'A million came from Europe, but a million British people have gone into Europe. You do know that there's a lot of British people staying in Europe as well?'

With that he ducked quickly into his official car, not realising his microphone to a national television broadcaster was still live.

'That was a disaster. Should never have put me with that woman – whose idea was that?' Brown demanded of an aide.

'I don't know, I didn't see her.'

'It's just ridiculous.'

'What did she say?' asked the aide.

'Ugh, everything – she's just some sort of bigoted woman. Said she used to be Labour. It's just ridiculous!'

Hugh guffawed when the recording was played back across all channels on the evening news, alongside pictures of Brown with his head in his hands when he'd first heard of the recording – a picture that came to define the election campaign. The whole incident became known as Bigotgate, and underlined just how out of touch politicians in Westminster had become.

'Serves the Scottish git right,' Hugh said to his new flame the next day, as they drove up to Lincolnshire in his Range Rover to introduce her to his ageing parents. Maria was a vivacious woman with auburn hair, hazel eyes and large round spectacles to combat her short sight.

Hugh was finally getting serious about a relationship and wondering if he should give up Westminster to take on the running of the farm. His father had already hired a manager as he could no longer cope on his own, and Hugh felt a bit guilty about being an absentee landlord. *Maybe one more election,* he thought. *I'm still a bit young to retire to the countryside.*

Maria was the daughter of a moderately successful West End actor called Ian, and she had no airs and graces, unlike most of Hugh's previous catches. He'd already met her parents, who lived in a modest semi-detached Victorian house in Richmond-upon-Thames, when they had lunched al fresco on Wiener schnitzels and proper German potato salad at a riverside restaurant. They'd carefully avoided much talk of politics, which Hugh was glad about because he suspected most actors were socialists, although he was surprised when Maria's father referred to Gordon Brown as a 'rotten puritan of the worst kind'.

Ian had also revealed that Maria had been so named after he and her mother, Louisa, had watched *West Side Story* during Louisa's pregnancy. 'Bit of a stupid name, really, I suppose,' he reflected, 'but there you go; we do some stupid things when we're young.'

'I never saw *West Side Story*,' Hugh said. 'Wasn't it basically an American rewrite of *Romeo and Juliet* with New York gangs instead of the Capulets and Montagues?'

'Pretty much. Maria was Juliet, and the song "Maria" stuck in my mind. Like I say, daft.' He glanced at Louisa.

'I never really liked the name,' Louisa said. 'Sorry, darling, should have put my foot down.' She reached out and covered her daughter's hand with her own.

Maria laughed. 'It's all right. Not many people mistake me for a Puerto Rican or a Filipino.'

'This potato salad is epic!' Hugh changed the subject.

'They import it direct from Germany,' Ian informed him.

'Why can't we make it like that?'

Overall, the lunch had been a success.

'So you think the Tories have got a chance, do you?' Maria asked now, as she looked in the vanity mirror and added a touch of lipstick.

'We've got a lot of baggage to lose; it'll be tight, but yes, I think we can win. Although I'm not sure about Cameron. He doesn't exactly exude charisma.'

'I can't think of a politician who does, to be honest. Except maybe that Nigel Farage.'

'Farage? A flash in the pan, surely?'

'Maybe, maybe not. He's full of surprises. And he *does* have the common touch, something severely missing in Westminster.'

'Hmm. Got to say, I hadn't given it too much thought. Maybe I should. Here we are, then,' Hugh announced as they pulled into the driveway that led up to the stone façade of his parents' double-fronted Georgian house. 'Gin and tonics all round, probably, but just relax; it'll be fine.'

'I am relaxed. I'm not worried about a thing.' She leaned over and gave Hugh a kiss on the cheek. '*You* relax!'

Maria was right about Farage, whose UK Independence Party won the second highest share of the UK vote in the elections for the European parliament in 2009. And Hugh was right about the 2010 general election, when Labour lost ninety-one seats, the biggest loss by Labour since 1931, and the result was a hung parliament.

Hugh had misgivings when the smooth-talking Cameron, yet another old Etonian, patched up a coalition government with Nick Clegg's Liberal Democrats, the country's first coalition government since World War Two. He thought Clegg was wetter than wet, like most in his party, and totally untrustworthy, but Cameron and Clegg seemed to get on with each other. They were both forty-three years old, and both came from wealthy and privileged backgrounds, which probably helped.

Nevertheless, Hugh's fortunes took an upturn again when he became a junior minister in the Home Office once more, tasked with helping to cut half a million jobs from the public sector workforce and clamp down on welfare payments as part of Chancellor George Osborne's five-year austerity programme, a mission he approached eagerly. He was less happy with Cameron's refusal to cut taxes and his attempts to shed the Tories' right-wing image. Hugh felt they weren't right-wing enough, and was tempted to defect to Farage's UKIP.

He was also horrified when Cameron enthusiastically joined the French president, Nicolas Sarkozy, in initiating bombing attacks on Colonel Muammar Gaddafi's Libya. The media loved it and egged on what they called the 'Arab Spring', but it quickly descended into chaos across the Middle East and led to the rise of the Islamic State, ISIS, in Syria.

Neither did Hugh think much of Cameron legalising same-sex marriage, or the way he referred to UKIP as 'fruitcakes, loonies and closet racists'. Especially when UKIP went on to win 20% of the vote in local elections in 2013, and then a year later won more votes than any other UK party in elections for the European parliament, gaining twenty-four seats.

In the general election in 2015, Cameron surprised everyone, including himself, by winning a ten-seat majority. Labour, led by the cringeworthy Ed Miliband, who was lampooned after struggling to eat a bacon sandwich on the campaign trail, slumped to their lowest number of seats since 1987, and the Scottish Nationalists became the third biggest party at Westminster, winning fifty-six of the fifty-nine Scottish seats. The Liberal Democrats almost disappeared, winning only eight seats, and Nick Clegg returned to the wilderness whence he'd come. Cameron promptly introduced his bill for a referendum on EU membership to fulfil a campaign manifesto promise.

The referendum on Scottish independence came and went the same year, with the nationalists soundly beaten, but the referendum over EU membership in 2016 soon loomed. As Cameron trundled back and forth to Brussels trying to win concessions to help him with the referendum, and failing at every attempt, the populist Conservative MP Boris Johnson goaded him from the sidelines, issuing statements and writing articles in support of Brexit.

'I think Cameron's goose might be cooked,' Hugh observed to the newly pregnant Maria at their new ground-floor garden apartment just off Kensington High Street. They had married on a freezing Saturday in February at the registry office in Richmond, with Miles as Hugh's best man. They had brought the wedding forwards because Hugh's parents were in obvious decline. Maria had put her job as an interior designer on hold for an indefinite time; she wanted to get through childbirth and then spend some time just being a mother. Neither she nor Hugh were young parents, which meant they felt they needed to devote as much time as possible to the baby; time suddenly seemed precious.

'Why do you say that?' Maria asked.

'Just take a drive outside the M25. It's all Brexit, Brexit, Brexit. I mean, if you listen to the media inside their London bubble, you'd think the Brexit vote has no chance. But it's different outside, especially as you go further north. I think a lot of people might also just welcome the chance to stick two fingers up to Westminster. But the media only listen to themselves; they're a bloody disgrace, really. The BBC, the *Guardian* and the so-called *Independent* are the worst.'

'You really think the Brexiteers might win?'

'I don't know for sure, but it's going to be very close, I can tell you. People are actually sick of being dictated to by Brussels, and, as you once said, that Farage really does come across as a man of the people. Always got a pint of beer in one hand and a cigarette in the other. People like him, they identify with him. And Boris is popular too.'

Johnson finally got off the fence and threw his considerable weight behind the Brexit campaign, and, sure enough, the pollsters and the mainstream media all went into deep shock when more than 17 million voters decided to leave the EU, winning the referendum by 52% against the 48% who wanted to remain in a federal Europe.

As much as anything, it was a poke in the eye for all the main political parties. In addition to the government, Labour, the Scottish

National Party, the Welsh Plaid Cymru, the Liberal Democrats and the Green Party had all campaigned for Remain. The British people thought otherwise, and David Cameron resigned, to be replaced as Conservative leader by the ineffectual Theresa May in July 2016 after Boris Johnson dropped out of the race, something that left Hugh aghast.

'She's hopeless, completely out of her depth!' he exploded. 'It's the worst possible decision.'

'Well, she has said "Brexit means Brexit" and that no deal is better than a bad deal,' Maria pointed out.

'Hmm. We'll see.'

CHAPTER TWENTY-NINE

A NATIONAL SCANDAL

'Thank heavens we're out of all that shit,' Miles said to Delen as they watched what passed for the evening news on the television.

'It's just appalling,' she said. 'How come nobody did anything about it for so long? What's the point of the police and social services these days?'

More revelations of mostly ethnic Pakistani Muslim 'grooming' gangs were just coming to light all over the country. It was first exposed in Rotherham, then Oxford, Huddersfield, Rochdale, Telford, and now it seemed to be in almost every town in England, Scotland and Wales.

'Why do they call them "grooming" gangs?' Miles asked. 'Surely grooming is when you take the dog for a haircut and to get his nails clipped? This is just evil; they're rape gangs. Christ, I hate the media, they're just complicit. I'm never paying that TV tax again. In fact, switch it off; it just makes me angry.'

The Rotherham so-called grooming gangs were the biggest failure in child protection in UK history. Local authorities and the police refused to act on reports of the abuse of hundreds of children, who were plied with drugs and alcohol, and even had petrol poured on them and were threatened with being burned alive. The victims were nearly all white, but there were also a fair number of Sikhs and children of other backgrounds targeted. In all, it was estimated that more than 1,400 children were abused over several decades in Rotherham, but it was just the tip of the iceberg. One survivor of the Rotherham abuse, under the name of Ella Hill, estimated that at least half a million non-Muslim girls had been raped over a period of forty years. The Home Office, when it finally investigated, was reluctant to publish its findings, because the reality didn't fit the narrative they wanted. 'The wrong victims and the wrong perpetrators,' as one commentator succinctly put it.

'And why do they keep calling them British Pakistanis?' Miles persisted. 'You're either one or the other; you can't be both, fucking media.'

'I suppose they have British passports? And the media are terrified of upsetting the "new British",' Delen suggested.

'So what? That doesn't make them English, or Scottish, or Welsh. They never can be, just like someone from Yorkshire can never be Cornish. It's not rocket science.'

'You know the Koran advocates the raping of infidel girls, don't you?' Delen was still watching the TV news bulletin. She flipped open her laptop and started searching.

'Seriously?'

'Yup, here it is, verses 4:3, 4:24, 23:6, and 33:50. Verse 65:4 also emphasises that Muslims can have sex with underage girls. Nice people, huh?'

'Makes me sick. Why do they let all these people in? They bring bugger all, and they don't want to integrate anyway, nor do most of us either, I suspect. We're told they "enrich" us, but why can't they enrich their own countries? Multiculturism will never work; has it worked anywhere?' Miles stood up to fetch a beer from the fridge. 'Fancy one?'

'Not to my knowledge, in answer to the first question. And no, I'm fine, thanks, in answer to the second, but you could check on Piran.'

Miles crept up the stairs and quietly peeked in at his son, fast asleep under his Batman duvet. His black curly hair was getting out of control, and Miles made a mental note to organise a trim. He also wondered if Piran's ears stuck out a bit too much.

Downstairs, he opened a bottle of local IPA. The news had moved on to 'institutional racism' in the Metropolitan police force. 'Hell's bells, it's unrelenting. Can you please switch it off, or put something more cheerful on?'

Delen reached for the remote and changed over to Netflix, and they began to watch a comedy about fraudsters on cruise ships.

*

Vic and Annabelle were feeling the same way as Miles and Delen.

'Reading was always a bit shabby, but not like it is now,' Vic complained. 'Curry houses everywhere, and I don't even like the stuff; litter everywhere; not a white cab driver in sight any more. Might as well be living in Lahore.'

'Mmmm.' Annabelle flicked through a magazine, barely paying him any attention. The subject had become something of a constant theme and she'd heard it all before. 'Well, do something about it, then. Moaning all the time isn't going to change anything.'

'Do what?' Vic sat up as the late afternoon sky darkened and the first few drops of rain spattered against the French windows.

They'd given up on the letter bombs after sending them out half a dozen times. Several civil servants had been injured, though none seriously, and the police had poured resources into hunting down the letter senders without success. If they'd carried on, though, sooner or later someone would have made a mistake, and the possible repercussions were unthinkable now that they had Alice to consider.

In fact, one of their members *had* made a mistake, by not using gloves when posting his letter. A fingerprint had been picked up, and Detective Inspector Parker thought Christmas had come early when the fingerprint showed up on the national database. The offender, who had a record for petty theft, had been hauled in for questioning. He was happy to tell all, but that wasn't much, as all he could give was a description of a blonde woman in a headscarf and dark glasses, and a ginger-headed man in a hat who never spoke. The descriptions had been given out to the media, and Annabelle had responded by cutting all links with the group. The trail had gone cold.

'Direct action is the only way in the end; you know that,' Annabelle said without looking up. 'But aren't we getting a bit past it for all that? I mean, I can't see you marching in the street and getting into brawls any more.'

'Yeah, sad, isn't it? But, you know, I haven't forgotten about Westminster. I've not told you, but I've been stockpiling stuff there for months now, tiny amounts at a time so no one notices; you can't just walk in with ten-gallon drums of the stuff.'

'What stuff?' She put the magazine down on the coffee table and stared at him.

'Petrol, mostly; what do you think? And some fuses. You know, stuff like that.'

'You're kidding me!'

'Well, no, I'm not. It's just in case it's needed one day, I look on it like an insurance policy.'

Annabelle laughed. 'Oh my, you *are* full of surprises!' She heard the key in the front door. 'There's Alice, right on time, which means it's time for a drink too, don't you think?'

Alice walked into the living room, her hair dripping, damp patches on the shoulders of her maroon school blazer, her grey skirt regulation knee-length. 'Hi, guys, what's for dinner? Smells delicious.'

'A bit early yet, isn't it? But roast chicken, since you ask. And Brussels sprouts.'

'Brussels sprouts?' Alice made a face.

'Only joking. Roast potatoes, carrots and peas, of course. How was your day?'

'Okay, I guess. We played soccer and I scored a goal.'

'Football,' Vic interrupted.

'Sorry?'

'It's called football. Only the Yanks call it soccer.'

'Oh, right. Football, then. But I've got loads of homework.'

'You want to do it before or after dinner?' Annabelle asked.

'Bit of each, I think, but I don't have to finish it all today. I'm going for a shower, then I'll make a start. How long have I got?'

'Oh, a good hour and a half. Dad is just going to make me a drink, aren't you, darling?'

'What? Oh, yes, of course. What'll it be?'

'I'm feeling naughty, so a vodka martini with a twist of lime... shaken, not stirred, of course, as Mr Bond would say,' she replied with a grin as Alice disappeared upstairs. 'What an amazing daughter we've produced. How did we do that?'

CHAPTER THIRTY

Terror on the Home Front

Hugh's elderly parents died within three months of each other. His mother went first after a fall down the stairs of their home, and then his father just seemed to give up and followed her to the grave after a heart attack while watching television. The daily help found him the next day, a half-finished bowl of peanuts and the remains of a gin and tonic by his side.

They were buried side-by-side at the local Anglican church. They had at least had the good fortune to witness the birth of their grandson, a bundle of energy with rosy cheeks and Hugh's fair hair, who had been named Dominic Ian in honour of his respective grandfathers.

Hugh and Maria sat in the living room of the old manor house, a fire burning low in the grate, while Maria rocked Dominic to sleep. Earlier they had walked through the fields full of sheep, while the farm manager told them about that year's bumper crop of barley and sugar beet, and how Lincolnshire was the provider of one eighth of the country's food.

'You know, maybe we should live here,' Maria said, out of nowhere. 'It's a beautiful place – well, it could be, needs a bit of work on the house, but after all it's been in your family for over two hundred years. You can't just sell up, can you?'

Hugh looked at her with astonishment. 'Are you serious? I've been wondering what to do about it. It would seem a bit of a betrayal to just get rid of it, but could you really live here? I mean, it's a bit remote.'

'Look, it's just three hours down the motorway to London, so it's not *that* remote. Only two hours by train from Lincoln to King's

Cross. And you did say you were thinking of giving up on the politics. I could put up with it for two or three years, the commuting, although it's true I wouldn't want to spend too much time here on my own. Might be a bit spooky.'

'Yes,' Hugh admitted, 'I am getting a bit fed up with Westminster. It's such a snake pit. And look at Miles and Delen; they seem so happy out in the countryside, and Cornwall really is a bit remote.'

Maria pushed her hair back, then stood slowly, so as not to disturb Dominic, and placed him in his cot. 'You don't like Theresa May, then?'

'I don't trust her. "Treason" May, some are calling her. And she's making a pig's ear of the Brexit negotiations. First she said she wanted a hard Brexit, WTO terms if needs be, but since she called her snap election in the summer and lost a bunch of seats to that lefty loon Jeremy Corbyn, she's been making concession after concession. And now we have to rely on the Democratic Unionists in Northern Ireland to be sure of winning any crucial votes. It's hopeless.'

'Corbyn reminds me of Steptoe.'

'The old rag and bone man?'

'Yes, the very same. And it seems that a lot of people are trying to undermine Brexit. Aren't they calling for another referendum?' Maria had gone to the drinks trolley, where she poured a glass of red wine for herself and a brandy for Hugh.

'Yes, so much for democracy,' he grunted, accepting the brandy. 'So they don't like the result of the vote, and want people to keep voting until the result suits them. It's like communism.'

'Well, maybe not that bad.'

'Not far off. Doesn't matter whether you wanted Remain or Leave to win; the result is the result and should be respected.'

Maria sat down again and sipped her drink thoughtfully, pushing a strand of hair behind her ear. 'You know, another reason I think I might be ready to move is that London has become quite unpleasant. All the big cities, really, what with all the terrorist attacks.'

In May 2017 a suicide bomber had attacked a pop concert with American singer Ariana Grande in the Manchester Arena, killing twenty-two people and injuring dozens more. Then, days before the June snap election, a van was driven into pedestrians on London Bridge, and the three occupants ran into Borough Market stabbing people randomly, killing eight people and injuring forty-eight others before they were shot dead.

'Yes, it's grim, isn't it? And don't forget poor Lee Rigby, hacked to death by a couple of Nigerians outside his barracks in Woolwich. That was horrific. But it seems to have been memory-holed, unlike that Stephen Lawrence; they're still banging on about that even though it was more than twenty years ago, his mother was made a dame and we even have a national day named after him. I guess maybe because he was black, fits the modern-day narrative.'

Maria laughed, digging Hugh in the ribs. 'You're sounding like quite the racist!'

'Hmm. Well, I never was, and I'm not, in fact, but there does seem to be a lack of balance. It's no good coming here and then calling us all racists. If I went to live in Africa or India, I'd respect their rules. We need a bit of that here, that's all I'm saying. And I don't like that mayor of London, Sadiq Khan; he's a race baiter if you ask me, always playing the race card.'

'Okay, okay, enough… but you know his dad was a bus driver in London? So I guess he is British, in a way.'

'As he keeps telling us. Probably drove like he was still in Islamabad or wherever.'

'You really are in a mood this evening!'

'No, I'm okay.' Hugh finished his brandy and stood to fetch another. 'I tell you what, let's think on this idea of moving here. In the meantime, the manager can look after the place. How about we go to visit Miles and Delen, just to get away for a few days? It might clear our minds.'

'I like that idea. Will you give them a call? No time like the present.'

'I'll do it right now.'

CHAPTER THIRTY-ONE

A Cornish Holiday

'Miles, old chum, how are you doing? How's life in the sticks?' Vic leaned back in his office in Vauxhall. His blond hair was thinning, but it was still there, and he'd let it grow long, covering most of his ears in an unruly mop. He was wearing his usual blue jeans, chequered shirt and work boots and watching Annabelle sort through some files.

It wasn't much of an office, truth be told, a brand-new Portakabin on a patch of wasteland they'd taken on a long rental, but it was comfortable, practical and cheap, with double-glazed windows, air conditioning and plenty of parking. The only downside was the regular rumble of the trains running in and out of Waterloo, but they had got used to that and barely noticed the noise by now.

Stuck to a whiteboard on the wall, Vic still had his ancient list of former colonies, now yellowed and torn in parts and covered in black lines as the former colonies had tumbled like dominoes. Antigua, Belize, Brunei, Dominica, Grenada, Hong Kong, Kiribati, Saint Lucia, Saint Kitts, the Grenadines, the Seychelles, the Solomon Islands, the Bahamas, Tonga and Zimbabwe had all gone. So had Anguilla, but they had changed their minds in 1971 and returned to the fold, and Bermuda had voted against independence. These two, along with Gibraltar, the Falkland Islands and South Georgia, were the only bits of red now left on Vic's world map.

'Vic? This is a surprise... to what do I owe the favour?' In contrast to the patch of wasteland in Vauxhall, Miles had his bare feet up on the wooden balcony of the sports centre on Carbis Bay beach, watching the swimmers, paddleboarders and canoeists in the glittering sea through his sunglasses. The surf was too low for surfboards.

'Ah, well, surprise surprise, I suppose. Annabelle and I have decided to take a short holiday, we need a break, so we've booked one of those cabins by the Carbis Bay Hotel on the beach. They look pretty good, hot tub, barbecue, the works. We're bringing Alice with us; she can miss the last few days of uni before the summer holidays, and hopefully we'll avoid the worst of the crowds. So we'll see you in a couple of days – if that's all right, of course?'

Miles sat up. 'Have you been talking to Hugh?'

'Hugh? The MP guy? No, why?'

'Must be psychic, then. He just called at the weekend. They're all coming down as well – in fact, he's probably on the road right now – so brilliant! All the kids together, buckets and spades, sandcastles, all that.'

'Alice is a grown-up already, so probably no bucket and spade. She's quite the lady, in fact! She's doing us a favour just by coming.'

'Huh, yes, I guess they're all getting a bit old for that now. Amazing how quickly time flies. Anyway, it is getting quite busy here already, but Carbis Bay is always okay; manageable, anyway. It's not like Porthia – sorry, St Ives. That's crawling with emmets already.'

'Emmets?'

'Sorry again, more Cornish slang. It's what we call outsiders, the tourists. I think it means ants.'

'So I'm a bleeding "emmet" now, am I?'

Miles laughed and stood up. He was looking at a couple of paddleboarders who seemed way too far out, but at least they were wearing lifejackets. 'No, 'course not! You'll be honorary Cornish folk while you're here. Want me to book the Beach Club Restaurant?'

'Definitely. Make it for the night after we arrive; it's a long drive, so Thursday? My shout.'

'Can't wait to see you then,' Miles told him. 'Give our love to Annabelle.' He hung up and told a colleague to watch the paddleboarders, then went inside the cabin to look for Delen, who was sorting wetsuits out. Piran and their daughter Wenna, born three years after her brother, also dark-haired and a bag of mischievous delight, were both still at school.

'Well, looks like we're in for a busy few days, then,' Miles said. He told Delan about Vic and Annabelle – and Alice.

'But that's wonderful!' Delen looked around from the rack, where she was trying to organise the wetsuits by size. 'I'll need to go shopping. And get cooking.'

'Don't worry about Vic and Annabelle; they've booked one of the chalets on the beach here. And we're eating out at the Beach Club on Thursday. I'll go and make sure we get a nice window table.'

As Miles headed off along the beach to sort out the restaurant bookings, Hugh and Maria were stuck in a traffic jam on the A303 approaching Stonehenge. It was a hot day; Hugh's pale spindly legs stuck out from his khaki shorts, and he wore an old purple Ralph Lauren polo shirt which had seen better days. Maria contrasted his scruffy holiday look with a loose yellow and white ankle-length designer print dress and designer sandals. The Range Rover's air conditioning was going full blast as Dominic slept with his mouth open on his booster seat in the back, a thin trail of drool running down to his chin, like a miniature version of an old man. On the CD the tales of Narnia had reached the end of the second story, *Prince Caspian*, and *The Voyage of the Dawn Trader* was about to start.

'I think we can turn that off now,' Maria said, ejecting the CD. 'He's asleep.' She put Classic FM on instead, and turned the volume down. 'That's better.' She leaned back.

'Hmm,' Hugh grunted. 'This is mad, the main road to the southwest and it's still a single carriageway. Look at the traffic!'

'How come they don't build something bigger, widen it or something?' Maria took off her glasses and looked out of the window as she polished them. The countryside was all blurred, like an impressionist painting, until she put her glasses back on and everything sprang back into focus.

'There are plans for a tunnel, but it's complicated. Whatever the government proposes, the eco loons start objecting, World Heritage site and all that. Which is fair enough in a way; Stonehenge is priceless, it has to be protected, but there must be a sensible solution.'

'There it is!' Maria said, sitting up and pointing across Hugh to the circle of prehistoric stones on Salisbury Plain. 'They look so small from here.'

'Maybe, but some of those stones weigh twenty-five tons. Makes you wonder how they got them here, and from where.'

'I read that they may have come from Wales. Maybe they brought them by boat part of the way, and then up from the coast?'

'We'll never really know, I guess,' Hugh said, glancing to his right. 'You know the whole monument is aligned toward the sunrise on the summer solstice? It's amazing, really. Some people think maybe it was some sort of burial ground.'

'Anyway, it's a real icon,' Maria concluded. 'It does need to be protected.'

'I guess, but still, this road is absolutely hopeless. Ah, there we go, we're moving again,' he said, as people who had slowed down to gawp at the national treasure started to accelerate again at last. 'Watch out for the novichok!'

'Eh?'

'We're on Salisbury Plain. Salisbury is where the Russians poisoned that old spy and his daughter with novichok, remember?'

'Oh, right. You do think of the weirdest things sometimes.'

Not long after, they negotiated huge roadworks where the road *was* being widened, and soon hit the A30, bypassing Truro and entering the joy of a dual carriageway. A little later, they were on the Hayle/Heyl bypass and took a right at the next roundabout, which was signposted Carbis Bay/Porthreptor.

'Hayle or Heyl?' Maria had asked as they'd passed the sign which showed both names.

'Hayle if you're English and Heyl if you're Cornish, I think,' Hugh said. 'But they both sound the same anyway. Unlike Carbis Bay and Porthreptor, or Porthia and St Ives.'

'There seem to be lots of Porths.'

'Yes, there are. I seem to remember Miles saying it meant "cove" or "bay" or something like that. Makes sense.'

They passed through Lannanta/Lelant, with its rows of houses all in Cornish stone, and past the Badger Inn to Carbis Bay itself.

'Now, according to the GPS we're almost there,' Hugh said. 'Yes, here we are: past Tesco on the corner, then turn left before the pub and up the hill a bit, at the end of a cul-de-sac. Yes, this is it.' He entered a short but wide driveway and stopped the car, and immediately Dominic woke up with the lack of movement and started gurgling. Hugh sounded his horn. 'At least I hope it's the right one!

It was a traditional Cornish cottage, double-fronted, with a slate roof and thick walls made from local granite. The door opened and Delen came out with a big smile. She was wearing a blue apron and her hands were covered with flour, which didn't stop her giving both Hugh and Maria big hugs, leaving white hand marks on their backs.

'Oh, sorry about that,' she said, dusting them off. 'Miles will be back any minute; he's always a bit late at this time of year. As long as the sun's out, people will play in the water. How was the drive?'

'Not too bad, just over six hours from South Kensington with a couple of coffee stops and Hugh being grumpy about the road,' Maria answered. She pushed her hair back and breathed deeply. 'Goodness me, it smells so clean and salty after London!' From the front garden they could see over the rooftops of the houses in the street below to a glimpse of the sea, as far as the Heyl estuary and the town's famous miles of golden sandy beach. She went to the back of the car to unbuckle Dominic, who was waving his arms, feeling ignored. 'Come here, big fella, come and say hello to Auntie Delen.'

'Auntie? Makes me sound old,' Delen said, laughing. 'Come on in, the kids are in the garden. I'm just finishing off a pie, steak and ale. Hope you haven't turned veggie?'

'No chance, not as long as the Pope's a Catholic,' Hugh said as he fetched their bags from the car boot.

'*Is* the Pope a Catholic?' Delen asked cheekily. 'Can't be too sure these days, I'm fairly certain the Archbishop of Canterbury isn't an Anglican, or maybe he's not even a Christian.'

'Hmm, you got that right!'

They stepped indoors, and Maria marvelled at the wooden ceiling beams in the lounge to the right (which were fortunately not so low that Hugh had to stoop), the fireplace, and the beautiful rugs that they'd spread over the oak floor. 'My God, it's amazing. You'd never really guess from the outside; I thought it'd be much smaller, and it's so cosy!'

'It gets better,' Delen told her. 'This way.'

To the left of the front door was the dining room, then Delen led them down the hallway to the kitchen with its Aga range, past the downstairs cloakroom, and through a door that opened onto an ample garden, which stretched to at least sixty feet.

'Piran, Wenna, come and say hello!'

The children got up from their sun loungers, where they'd been engrossed in their phones, and sauntered over.

At the bottom of the garden was an outbuilding, too smart for a shed, with large glass windows at the front. 'Your annex,' Delen said. 'It's a bit small, but it's got a king-size bed and an ensuite with a shower, and there's Wenna's old cot, so you'll be fine. And the back door is always open if you need.'

'That's divine!' Maria said. 'But you leave your door open? Aren't you worried about thieves?'

'No, it's not like that down here, and the neighbour has a dog. We never have any trouble. We built the annex last winter so Miles' mum Molly can stay over sometimes; she's getting old and doesn't like to drive any more. Now go and get settled in, and we'll see you when you're ready.'

Miles came home half an hour later and took Hugh off to the Cornish Arms to catch up, while the women fussed in the kitchen, Delen putting the finishing touches to the pie and Maria peeling vegetables.

'A woman's place is in the kitchen, eh?' Hugh joked once they were safely out of earshot.

CHAPTER THIRTY-TWO

The Beach Club

Vic, Annabelle and Alice were waiting for the rest of them when they walked into the Beach Club Restaurant two days later. Both Hugh and Vic already had bright red necks and arms from the sun, while the more sensible Annabelle and Maria revealed just a healthy glow, and Miles and Delen bore the deep bronzed tans of perpetual beachgoers.

The table was next to the huge picture window right above the beach, and a high chair had been placed for Dominic at the far end of the table, surrounded by Alice, Piran and Wenna. The tide was in, so the sea was only a few yards away from the building; the sun was still high and the turquoise water sparkled.

'Hey, here we are again!' Vic put his Bloody Mary down, and he and Annabelle stood to embrace Delen, Maria, Miles and Hugh in turn. 'Lucky we're not frogs, or I'd have to give you all five kisses and all.'

They ordered two bottles of Picpoul, which was one of their favourite white wines, and soft drinks for the children. Alice was allowed a glass of wine, which she watered down.

'So, this is your latest one?' Vic pointed at Wenna. 'What's her name again? She's a cutie.'

Wenna scowled and went bright red.

'Wenna,' said Delen. 'It means "white", though it's also the name of another local saint.'

'White, huh? Better not tell some of our new neighbours.' Vic chuckled at his own joke, though nobody else did, and Annabelle trod on his foot under the table.

'Behave yourself,' she admonished him.

'Well, this is fun. Cheers, everyone!' Hugh toasted them, and they all raised their glasses.

'That's my office there.' Miles pointed down the beach to where the wooden building of the sports centre sat a hundred yards away. 'That's where I spend my working days.'

'Blimey, beats Vauxhall,' Vic said. 'I'll have to come down and hire a canoe or something tomorrow.'

'On the house, mate. What about you, Annabelle? Are you going to venture into the sea?'

'I've always fancied trying a paddleboard, but I really don't like the cold. What if I fall in? How warm is it?' she asked, looking up from the menu.

'Warm? Ah, it's never *that* warm, it's the North Atlantic, but it was a blistering sixteen degrees centigrade today…'

'Sixteen degrees? That's freezing!'

'Don't worry, we'll get you a wetsuit. And a lifejacket. You'll be fine. In a couple of weeks' time we've got the Celtic Cup happening here, biggest paddle boat event in the country, kayaks, outrigger canoes, the lot; it'll be teeming.'

'Well, fish and chips for me, I reckon. It's got to be good here!' Vic announced as the waitress came to take their orders.

Miles ordered a selection of warm bread with olive oil and balsamic vinegar, olives, crispy fried squid and pan-fried scallops for them to pick over while they waited for their main courses.

'Tell me,' Hugh asked Vic, 'how's the work going? At parliament, I mean.'

'Oh, you don't want to know, mate.' Vic shook his head as he speared a scallop with his fork. 'It's a horror story. You should come down and visit me there sometime, I'll show you around.'

'That bad?'

'You've no idea what you're sitting on. Still, if it does all go up, maybe we'd be rid of a few of the tossers. Present company excepted, of course. I mean, that Maybot is pathetic. The people in Brussels are running rings around her, Verhoftwat and Barnier, all unelected technocrats; we're a laughing stock.'

'Tell me about it,' Hugh grunted in acknowledgement.

'Well, if you ask me, she won't last long, then that Boris will take over,' Vic said. 'Maybe he'll sort them out. What do you think?'

'Honestly, I'm not sure I care any more. I'm thinking of chucking it in and standing down at the next election, which isn't that far off.'

Everyone looked at him, eating paused. 'Seriously?' asked Miles. 'I thought you were a politician for life.'

'So did I once, but not any more. Maria and I, we've been talking about it; we're thinking of becoming farmers. You know, since my parents died, and since Westminster turned into such a shitshow. I don't know, but we are thinking seriously about it. The farm is there, it's a beautiful place, and now we have Dominic to think about.'

'Wow!' said Delen as the others nodded. 'Do you know anything about farming? It's hard work.'

'Sure, I grew up on the farm, and we have a good manager; he'll help me settle in, teach me some of the ropes. I'd probably keep him on, anyway. And it's not all scythes and pitchforks these days; long days, yes, but it's easier than the old times. Except for the sheep. Plus first I need to sort out the death taxes; they're not cheap, but I think we can make it if we sell the London flat. The place has been in the family a long time, and I don't really want to live in London any more. It's becoming a bit Third World, if you know what I mean.'

'Too right,' Annabelle cut in, playing with her seafood linguine. A few grey strands were starting to show in her otherwise jet-black hair. 'I don't like London any more either; thank God we still have the place in Caversham. And the death tax is outrageous, taxing money that's already been taxed. It used to be for the super-rich only, but now it's anyone who owns a semi-decent flat in a semi-decent area of London.'

'We *are* the super-rich, darling,' Vic said with a smirk. 'Well, not billionaires, obviously, but even if they put the death tax threshold up to a million quid, we'll still get hit. Bastards.'

*

Vic's political predictions weren't too far off. Theresa May resigned in June 2019 after a disastrous couple of years. After calling her cabinet ministers down to Chequers the previous year to rally them around, she instead found herself facing some serious pushback from the European Research Group (ERG), who wanted to take a much harder line with Brussels. Her Brexit secretary David Davies resigned, complaining that she was giving away too much too easily, and he was followed within a day by Boris Johnson, who resigned as foreign secretary, saying the 'dream' of Brexit was dying and being 'suffocated by needless self-doubt'.

Nevertheless, Theresa May boasted in November that she had secured a withdrawal plan that 'delivered for the British people', which had been agreed by the other twenty-seven EU member countries. Except she hadn't obtained the agreement of the DUP, who were furious that her proposed backstop plan for Northern Ireland raised the spectre of regulatory barriers between the six counties and the rest of the UK.

Hugh was a small cog in the ERG and furiously paced the lounge of their South Kensington flat a week or so before Christmas when May narrowly survived a vote on her leadership of the Conservative Party, put forward by the ERG. 'It's just one disaster after another,' he raged. 'She has to go, one way or another.'

"Tis the season of goodwill to all men.' Maria stood in front of him, putting a stop to his pacing, and squinted up at him; she'd left her glasses on the coffee table. 'Come on, it's not the end of the world. Let's finish our packing and head up to Lincolnshire for a lovely Christmas and forget all this for a while.'

Hugh, as ever, was easily mollified. 'All right, yes, you're right. The sheep are more important.'

'Are you referring to the voters?' she teased, smiling.

Hugh put his arms around her and kissed her. 'You're beautiful, you know? And I love you dearly.'

'I do know, you silly old fool, of course I do.'

'Come on, then, let's finish that packing.'

*

It was Theresa May's last Christmas as Prime Minister. In January, she again narrowly survived a vote of confidence in parliament, tabled by Jeremy Corbyn after her Brexit agreement had been rejected. She desperately sought further concessions from Brussels, but they were playing hardball, sensing blood.

In March 2019 the House of Commons voted by 312 to 308 against leaving the EU without a deal. Two months later Nigel Farage's new Brexit Party won twenty-nine seats in the European parliament, against just four for the Conservatives, and May knew the game was up. Boris Johnson took over leadership of the party in July.

CHAPTER THIRTY-THREE

Atishoo, Atishoo, and We All Locked Down

'Alexander Boris de Pfeffel Johnson. What kind of a fucking name is that?' Vic asked rhetorically.

'He's Turkish, and another Eton prat,' Annabelle answered anyway. They were back in Caversham for the August bank holiday weekend. Across the river the Reading Festival was in full swing, the noise bouncing off their windows and sending Vic into one of his moods.

'Says here this Carrie what's-her-name is his third wife, but they got married in Westminster Cathedral, which is Catholic. So how can that be? Both his ex-wives are still alive, so I thought the Catholics didn't allow that. And he had four kids with his last wife.' He was sitting at the dining table, studying his laptop. He'd shaved his head after realising he was fighting a losing battle against impending baldness, and was enjoying the feeling of running a hand back and forth over the stubble. 'Christ, I wish they'd turn that bleeding bass down at least!'

'Boris probably doesn't think the rules apply to him,' Annabelle pointed out as she looked out of the window, not realising how prophetic her words would prove to be.

'Well, I suppose a Turk is better than a darkie, just about. But then I wouldn't be surprised to see one of them in Downing Street either before I pop my clogs. And at least Boris makes me laugh, the fat sod. Looks like Billy bleeding Bunter.' Vic had no idea that he too was being prophetic.

Boris became leader of the Conservatives and thus prime minister in July 2019, promising to 'get Brexit done'. But when he seemed ready to go for a 'no deal' departure from the EU, the House of Commons voted to force a delay of the British withdrawal until the end of January at the earliest. Boris then presented a renegotiated deal which looked pretty much identical to May's proposals, except the Northern Ireland backstop was replaced with a plan to keep the six counties aligned with EU regulations for four years from the end of any transition period.

With 'no deal' off the table, Jeremy Corbyn indicated he was finally ready to support an early election. Boris duly called one for 12th December, and won a stunning victory, again confounding the polls and the mainstream media. Many Labour 'red wall' voters in the Brexit-supporting north of the country switched sides for the first time that anyone could remember, and Boris returned to parliament triumphant, with an eighty-seat majority.

'This is the moment when the dawn breaks, and the curtain goes up on a new act in our great national drama,' Boris told the nation.

'Bollocks,' muttered Hugh, who hadn't stood for re-election. He had moved back to the family farm in Lincolnshire with Maria and Dominic.

'Don't you miss it?' Maria asked over a lunch of cold ham with new potatoes and leeks. 'No regrets?'

'None at all, believe it or not. This so-called agreement is a sham. He's ignored the DUP and basically given away our sovereignty in Northern Ireland. That's unforgiveable. And anyway, it'll take them forever to hammer out the final details of a new trade deal. And I bet he gives too much away. Boris may be fun and irreverent and a charmer, but he's intrinsically lazy and dishonest, in my view anyway.'

The decision to move out of London and back to the countryside proved to be a huge bonus when the world was hit by coronavirus, initially thought to have been released by mistake by the Wuhan Institute of Virology in China, though this was hotly disputed by China and never proven officially. Other scientists suggested it had been transmitted by bats. In the UK people referred to it as Chinese flu, until this was deemed 'racist', and in time it became known simply as Covid.

Alice had been on holiday in Thailand in October, and when Vic and Annabelle picked her up from Heathrow airport, she was very ill.

'I was fine when I got on the aeroplane,' she croaked as they got into Vic's Jaguar 4x4. 'Now I feel terrible, like it's a really bad flu.' She was hot and feverish and shivering at the same time, and had difficulty breathing.

'Aeroplanes. Terrible things for spreading any kind of germ or virus,' Annabelle said. 'Come on, let's get you home and tucked up in bed. It'll soon pass.'

It did pass, but it took ten days and copious amounts of Lemsip mixed with lemon, honey and a dash of whisky. At the end Alice was exhausted; her energy had gone, along with her sense of taste, although that came back some weeks later.

'That was the worst ever,' she said as she curled up on the sofa next to her mother. 'I hope you don't get it, wouldn't wish it on anyone.'

But they did; both Annabelle and Vic succumbed in quick succession, but both also recovered. The first cases of coronavirus had just been announced.

'Fuck me, we must have just had the chinky flu, then,' Vic announced. 'It's probably been around in Asia for months and poor Alice picked up a dose. Well, at least we've got immunity now.'

To begin with, scientific advisors said that the best way to limit the long-term effects was indeed to allow the virus to spread naturally and generate 'herd immunity', and to begin with Boris Johnson took a low-key approach to the problem, unlike the far more aggressive tactics deployed in much of the rest of the world, like Australia, New Zealand and Canada.

In March, though, with the virus continuing to spread even if the more traditional flu virus was said to have mysteriously disappeared, the UK government introduced 'social distancing', mask wearing and a nationwide lockdown, closing schools, pubs, restaurants and other businesses. Police were given powers to break up gatherings of more than two people, and everyone was told to stay at home except for going out to exercise once a day or for essential shopping. The government had started listening to doom quacks like Professor Neil Ferguson, a key member of SAGE, the government's Scientific Advisory Group for Emergencies, a man who had rarely been right about anything in the past and who ignored his own advice by conducting an affair during lockdown.

'This guy is a fucking maniac, completely loopy.' Vic was back on his laptop. 'Says here he was wrong about foot and mouth disease in 2001 when six million cattle were destroyed at a cost of six billion quid, even though there was no evidence of infection at farms neighbouring those who were infected. He was wrong about mad cow disease a year later when he said between 50,000 and 150,000 people would die, and only 117 actually did. He was wrong about bird flu in 2005 when he claimed 200 million people could die, and only 282 did. And he was wrong about swine flu in 2009 when he reckoned there would be 85,000 deaths, instead of the 457 who actually did die. Now he's saying millions could die from this Covid. He's an idiot if you ask me.'

'I doubt if anyone will ask you,' Annabelle, wearing an emerald green dress and smoking a rare cigarette, replied in her usual way. 'But I'm not having one of those vaccines, and neither is Alice. They've not been fully tested, can't have been in the time they've been rolled out.'

'Me neither; last time I had a flu vaccine was the last time I had flu. It's a virus, for Christ's sake, it changes all the time. Anyway, like I said before, I reckon we've got the best immunity now, 'cause we've had it. But some people will be making a lot of money out of this.'

'Remember thalidomide? People got rich out of that too.'

Every evening Vic and Annabelle went out under the cover of darkness to put stickers on lamp posts, shop fronts, car windows, any surface they could find, deriding the lockdown and the vaccines and the useless mask wearing, and tearing off the tape that council workers had put on park benches and playgrounds to supposedly protect people.

'Masks are for keeping germs in; they don't protect you from anything that's incoming,' Annabelle explained. 'It's a well-known fact. The Japanese have been wearing them for decades if they have a cold or flu or something; it's to keep your germs *in*, and you need to change them every day or wash them.'

The country began a nationwide clap for the NHS on Thursday evenings, while doctors and nurses made TikTok videos and 'Nightingale' emergency hospitals stood empty. Hundreds of thousands of people up and down the country, if not millions, stood at their front doors or on balconies clapping and banging pots and pans at eight o' clock every Thursday night for months.

'It's madness, like a mass psychosis has gripped the nation. What the fuck is going on? It's brainwashing; they're turning the useless NHS into some sort of religion or cult,' Vic fumed, although fortunately their house was sufficiently secluded that they didn't have to listen to the Thursday night cacophony.

Thousands of old people were moved out of hospitals into care homes without proper screening, and many died. The health secretary, Matt Hancock, was put in charge of the procurement of personal protective equipment with little competitive tendering, and pushed for more severe lockdowns until he was caught snogging his lover in his office and resigned.

'He's one of the bastards who's been getting rich on this scam,' Vic muttered, 'but he's not the only one, for sure.'

A variety of prominent media figures such as Andrew Neil, Piers Morgan, Nick Ferrari and Vanessa Feltz also pushed for more stringent lockdown or vaccination rules, some even suggesting that people who had refused to have the Covid vaccine should be denied NHS treatment in the event of illness.

'That fat fuck Ferrari should also be refused treatment then; obesity like that is a self-inflicted illness.' Vic was in a complaining mood again. 'And as for Penis Morgan, he's still got blood on his hands from the Iraq war, printing those fake pictures of squaddies allegedly torturing prisoners. How come they never get called to account?'

'Because they're part of the scam. But you're doing okay on the furlough scheme, though, aren't you, darling?' Annabelle pointed out as she set the table for lunch.

Chancellor Rishi Sunak had introduced the furlough scheme, under which the government picked up 80% of the wages of anyone in full-time employment who had to stay at home, to help businesses and their staff survive the lockdown, spaffing billions of pounds up the wall. Later, as lockdown was eased and pubs reopened, he would introduce his 'Eat Out to Help Out' scheme, subsidising meals out and costing another few billions' worth of taxpayers' money.

'For sure I'm claiming furlough, for me and all the staff, be mad not to,' Vic retorted. 'But the whole lockdown thing is bonkers. Sweden hasn't done it and they've had no more deaths than us, while our economy is in ruins, and this furlough thing is like everyone's on gardening leave; we're all being paid not to work. And people will get used to that, you'll see. It won't be so easy to get them back to the office.'

'I'm sure you're right. I think it's all an exercise in control, and it's working. And I don't believe Boris ever "nearly died" of Covid either; he just wasn't following orders and someone got at him. Two weeks after of his so-called near-death experience he was out partying. Now, gazpacho? And there's some garlic bread in the oven.'

Vic ambled over to the table, still muttering. 'Where's Alice?'

'She's gone for a run. She can eat when she comes home. It's not as if the gazpacho is going to get cold, given that it already is.'

'Very funny.'

'Oh, come on! Lighten up!'

'Sorry, I'm just going a bit stir crazy. Can't wait to get back to work, to be honest.'

As the pubs reopened, people were told they could take their masks off if they were sitting down, but had to be masked if standing up.

'Clown world,' Miles said. He, Delen and the children were

enjoying their first meal out in more than a year at the Gurnard's Head pub near Zennor, a few miles south of St Ives. Miles had also spent lockdown on furlough, as if swimming in the sea put you in danger of getting Covid. 'So what? Now the virus can only get you if you're standing up? But my favourite bit of propaganda was that having no symptoms is a symptom of Covid. I mean, for fuck's sake! So you feel just fine, which means you might be sick? How stupid do they think we are?'

'Very stupid,' Delen said. 'And the thing is, most people *are* stupid and very gullible. They bought into it, didn't they?'

Before lockdown was eased, the Duke of Edinburgh died just a couple of months short of marking his hundredth year, having spent nearly seventy-four of them married to Queen Elizabeth the Second. She cut a forlorn figure at his funeral, dressed in black and sitting alone in St George's Chapel in Windsor, while in Downing Street the previous night they had partied, as they had throughout lockdown. Boris really didn't seem to think the rules that he forced on everyone else applied to him, and 'Partygate' would lead to his downfall.

'Talk about hubris,' Delen remarked. 'Can't say he doesn't deserve everything coming his way.'

'But that Keir Starmer and the Labour lot were also having curry and beer nights. Not to mention those people at Sky News, Beth Rigby and Kay Burley and a few others.'

'Ah, yes, "Sly News". Well, I guess we'll find out that that's different; it always is. And the lefty media won't touch our Mr Quare Stormer.'

'Wasn't he head of the Crown Prosecution Service during the Rotherham rapes scandal? How did he get away with that?'

'Shhhh!'

CHAPTER THIRTY-FOUR

A STATUE IS TOPPLED

Hugh, Maria and Dominic were less affected by Covid than their friends; life on the farm continued pretty much as normal except for socialising, given that they were considered 'essential workers'. The country still had to eat, after all.

Dominic wasn't able to go to school, but at his age it was no huge loss. While he missed out on the company of other children, he enjoyed his tasks, feeding the chickens and collecting the eggs, riding on the tractor with his father, or watching the manager's sheepdog, Billie, round up the sheep.

'So, that Joe Biden actually got more than ten million votes more than Obama got when he was elected last time. Can you believe that?' Hugh asked when they heard the US presidential election results. They were having a simple lunch of ham, egg and cress sandwiches in the kitchen. Outside the rain was lashing down and the wind howling, the sheep were huddled together in the corners of their respective fields, and farming had been put on hold for the day.

'No.' Maria considered for a moment. 'It's all a bit fishy, really, how the numbers suddenly changed overnight when Trump was leading by a mile. Where did all those new votes suddenly come from, and can their counting machines be trusted?'

'Oh well, not really our problem. Except the old bloke seems to be another Brit hater. Probably won't end well.'

Dominic was busy on the floor trying to hammer a square peg into a round hole.

'Wonder how long it'll take him to work it out? Oh, there you go!' Maria said as Dominic finally did work it out. 'Mind you, I'm sure

I've seen videos of some animals doing it faster. You know, crows, rats, that sort of thing. We humans are a bit slow with the growing up bit.'

'And we never seem to learn from our mistakes; that's one thing you do learn from history.'

As it happened, in June Joe Biden made his first foreign trip as president to England, to attend the G7 summit in, of all places, Carbis Bay, resulting in a week of hell for Miles and Delen and other local residents. Thousands of police were drafted in, setting up checkpoints on the entry roads, bringing a massive increase in Covid infections with them, and making free movement all but impossible. Even the beach was declared strictly off limits as the police patrolled the sea in rigid boats.

Meanwhile, the leaders of Canada, France, Germany, Italy, Japan, the US and the UK bumped elbows, held photo ops and frittered away a few more million pounds of taxpayers' money as they supposedly discussed how to 'build back better' and create a greener, more prosperous world. Australia, India, South Korea and South Africa were also invited. But not China or Russia, as if they had no role to play in the world's future.

'You know, now I look at it from the outside, I can see what a detestable, incestuous affair the whole thing is,' Hugh observed as he watched the porpoise-like Boris Johnson wade into the sea for the cameras. 'I mean, when I was in Westminster, everyone there really seemed to think we were the centre of the universe. Even if half the MPs had never had proper jobs in their lives, they always seemed to think they knew better and had a duty to interfere in every tiny aspect of people's lives. Arrogant, hypocritical and mean-spirited, almost to a man. And woman. And the venal media just follow the rulebook unquestioningly; there's no real journalism any more.'

'You were a good MP,' Maria told him. 'For the constituents, anyway.'

'Maybe, maybe not. But when I went into politics, it was with good intentions. I wanted to serve my country, help to make it a better place.'

'A bit of a novel concept these days.' Maria was lying on the sofa reading *The Camp of the Saints*, a 1970s dystopian novel by French writer Jean Raspail, which described the destruction of Western civilisation by mass immigration from the Third World. She looked up over her glasses. 'I think the sole purpose of the state now is to spend vast amounts of money on problems that don't exist. Like climate change.'

'Climate change? Well, that does exist, doesn't it?'

'I don't know, to be honest. David Bellamy, the only naturalist I ever really respected, told us that global warming, or cooling, is part and parcel of the natural cycle, and there's nothing we can do to stop these cycles. So now we face spending enormous amounts of tax money trying to solve a problem that doesn't exist.'

'You don't think we should be cutting carbon emissions? Installing wind farms and solar panels, that sort of thing?'

'You forgot about killing all the cows, never mind that there used to be 60 million or so bison in America,' she answered wryly. 'But to answer your question, maybe we should be looking at alternative energy sources, but not necessarily wind farms or solar power. The trouble with wind farms is that when the wind is too strong, they don't work. And when there's not enough wind, they don't really generate much electricity. And they kill birds. And when their lifespan is up, how do we dispose of them? Same with solar panels. We're not exactly the sunniest of countries, but anyway they also have a limited lifespan and we don't know how to dispose of them either. As long as China and India are pumping out the carbon in ever-increasing amounts, I can't see what difference us closing a couple of coal mines will make to the world. We should maybe be looking at things like geothermal solutions, and in the meantime we should be fracking, like Trump did in America. We have vast shale deposits; we shouldn't be relying on other people for our energy.'

'Crikey, I think that's one of the longest speeches I've ever heard you make!' Hugh switched off the television; the news was depressing him.

'You should read this book,' Maria said. 'I think unfettered immigration is where our immediate real problem is going to come from. It might be fiction, but then so was *Nineteen Eighty-Four*, and look at us now. *Nineteen-Eighty-Four is* now.'

'That's the trouble with conspiracy theories,' Hugh joked. 'They keep coming true.'

*

Shortly before the Carbis Bay conference, an African American with a long criminal record, George Floyd, died when a police officer knelt on his neck for more than eight minutes during an arrest. Floyd was six feet and six inches tall, an imposing figure and a 'gentle giant' according to his friends. To the police, aware that he had served four years in prison for aggravated robbery with a deadly weapon, when he had pushed a gun into the abdomen of a woman whose house he and some friends were robbing, he was someone to be treated with caution. He'd also been arrested several other times on drug and theft charges. His autopsy later showed he was Covid positive, and had significant amounts of fentanyl and methamphetamine in his system, but they were ruled out as the cause of death, and the arresting police officer was charged with homicide.

The orgy of riots and looting that erupted across America in the wake of Floyd's death soon spread to the UK, with protests, supported by the Labour party and the SNP and often violent, in London, Manchester, Cardiff and other major cities. They occurred during a temporary easing of lockdown measures, but large gatherings were still supposedly banned.

In Bristol a mob toppled the Grade II listed statue of Edward Colston, a man who had made a significant portion of his fortune in the slave trade in the seventeenth century, but also someone who had given financial support to almshouses, hospitals, schools, workhouses and churches across England and especially in his home city of Bristol. The statue, by an Irish sculptor, had been erected in 1895. Once toppled, the mob threw the statue into the harbour, while the police, afraid of creating more disorder, watched on and did nothing.

Superintendent Andy Bennett of the Somerset and Avon Police said afterwards, 'We decided the safest thing to do was to allow it to take place.'

'Looks like the lockdowns are really basically self-imposed by suggestion and threats from the politburo, and some people are more equal than others, comrade,' Hugh remarked.

'Becoming quite the cynic, aren't we, dear?' Maria ribbed him.

'What's a junkie in America with a criminal record got to do with us?' Vic demanded of Annabelle a couple of hundred miles further south. 'I mean, shame that he died, but seriously, what the fuck has it got to do with us?'

'Just an excuse for a chimp-out,' Annabelle replied drily. 'It's all virtue signalling these days.'

Footballers across the country started 'taking the knee' at the beginning of matches in sympathy with the BLM movement.

'Bleeding mongs,' Vic muttered. 'Paid a fortune to kick an updated pig's bladder around and they think we actually care about their politics? Christ, what a shitshow. Am I supposed to feel guilty for being white?'

Annabelle didn't even bother giving an answer to that one.

CHAPTER THIRTY-FIVE

The Multicultural Dividend

Miles was in the back of the sports centre while Delen took over the watch from the balcony. The day was overcast, but the sea was as calm as a millpond. It was still not quite the high season; the year's Celtic Cup was still a couple of weeks away, and business was slow.

Three people had just been stabbed to death in Nottingham by an immigrant from Guinea-Bissau in west Africa, Valdo Calocane, who had entered the UK after being granted Portuguese citizenship. Two of the dead were promising young students at the university, the third a school caretaker. The assailant had then stolen a van and driven into pedestrians, and had injured three more people.

Miles was reading about the attack on his social media page. A cartoon popped up showing a group of politicians sitting around a table, with a huge elephant standing in the corner. A speech bubble from one of the politicians showed him saying, 'So, we'll go with mental health issues again, shall we?'

Miles grunted. 'That'd be funny if it wasn't so true,' he murmured.

He went to a search engine to look up the list of terror attacks since the Manchester Arena bombing, the bombings on the London tube trains, the London Bridge attack, and the murder of Fusilier Lee Rigby. It was a long list.

Miles read: *In 2017 Parsons Green tube station was bombed, with thirty injured. In November 2019, Usman Khan, the son of Pakistani immigrants convicted of plotting a terrorist attack in 2012, stabbed two of his Cambridge University rehabilitation volunteers to death and injured three others before being shot dead. The following January a prison officer at Whitemoor Prison was stabbed numerous*

Ames by Muslim inmates. A month after that, Saddesh Amman, of Sri Lankan parentage, was shot dead after stabbing two people in Streatham. In March, seven-year-old Emily Jones was stabbed to death in Bolton by an illegal Albanian immigrant. In Reading's Forbury Gardens, three people were stabbed to death and three more seriously injured by a Libyan refugee, Khairi Saadallah, who was arrested and received life imprisonment. In October 2021, Conservative MP David Amess was stabbed to death by Ali Harbi Ali, a Somali, while holding a constituency surgery. A month later, Emad al-Swealmean, a Syrian refugee who had been refused asylum but not removed from the country, tried to bomb the Liverpool Women's Hospital, but his bomb exploded in the taxi he was taking, killing him and wounding the driver. The police said they have foiled multiple other attacks.

Miles wandered out to the balcony and showed the list to Delen. 'Take a look at that,' he said. 'It's never-ending, makes you wonder when the next atrocity is going to happen.'

'It's not as if British people – I mean real British people – never murder anyone,' she pointed out.

'I never said that,' Miles retorted. 'But just because we have our own criminals, it doesn't mean we've got to import more riffraff from all over the world. And they're mostly Muslims; they don't integrate much, do they? What was it Churchill said? "When Muslims are the minority, they push for minority rights. But when Muslims are the majority, there are no minority rights." Kind of sums it up.'

'I've seen that somewhere too, but I'm not sure he actually ever said it. I think it was debunked.'

'Whether he said it or not, it sounds true.'

'And anyway, it's not just the Muslims causing trouble. Look at all the stabbings in London, more than eleven thousand knife crimes last year. Khan's paradise.'

'True, I think that's mostly black-on-black.' Miles punched the keys on his tablet. 'Says here 107 dead from stabbings in London last year. That's a big number!'

'There's not much we can do about it, though, is there?'

'That's just giving up! For a start we could defend our borders. Never mind the so-called legal immigration which added another million to the country last year; what about the dinghies in the Channel? Seven million quid a *day* we're paying to put these illegals up in hotels. The local staff are being sacked and replaced by Serco thugs, local communities are being wrecked. And we've got veterans sleeping in the street.'

Delen sighed. 'I know, I know, but there's no point in getting so worked up. I mean, we're kind of shielded from it here in Cornwall.'

'Not forever; it'll come here too. We've already got some hotels full of illegals. A girl was raped by one of them in Newquay a few weeks back, remember? And anyway, I *am* worked up about this. The politicians are lying to us, always saying they're going to stop it when in fact they're the ones facilitating it. I mean, the media and the left are always moaning about how we need more money for the NHS, more houses, more schools, more everything. But if you look between the lines, the utility companies all think the population is already nearer 80 million than the official 70-odd million. Of *course* we can't cope!'

'I don't understand where all the money comes from to pay for it all. And the war in Ukraine on top.'

'That's another madness, poking the Russian bear. But I guess they just keep printing more and taxing us more. It's all taxpayers' money in the end. *Our* money!'

'It seems to be the same everywhere: France, Germany, Italy, Spain. It's not just here.'

'And that's not an excuse, and you know it. In fact, it just makes it worse. We're seeing mass population replacement, and it's not good.'

'I'm not sure we're talking actual population replacement here.' Delen stood and stretched.

'What do you think, then?' Miles turned the tablet off and took his turn watching the few people out braving the sea.

'Maybe it's just divide and rule, the oldest trick in the book,' she suggested.

'You think? Well, either way, to me it looks more like a globalist plan, the World Economic Forum people. We've already got an Indian prime minister, while the Scots have got a Pakistani!'

'They're British!' Delen objected. 'And now you're sounding like a conspiracy theorist.'

'So you say, but isn't it handy that the billionaire Sunak has got a green card for when he needs it? He's only been an MP for a few years and suddenly he's prime minister. And funny that no one actually voted for him to be prime minister. His fellow MPs might have wanted him, but the Conservative Party members rejected him. Kicking out Liz Truss, however bad she was, looked like a soft coup to me. And bear in mind that this is the world that Piran and Wenna are going to inherit.'

'Talking of which, time for the school run,' Delen said, tiring of the conversation and grateful to find a way out.

'But they always walk home.'

'I know, but Wenna has a party to go to today, so I said I'd go and pick them up. Go for a swim, dear, clear your head, and I'll see you at home.'

CHAPTER THIRTY-SIX

A Very British Coup

A few months earlier, Vic had stomped into his Portakabin in Vauxhall, a red Trumpian MAGA baseball cap on his head, his jeans covered in dust and grease, his hands likewise. 'I *knew* it! What did I bleeding tell you?'

Annabelle, looking cool in a white cotton blouse and knee-length shorts which showed off her tanned legs, was catching up on emails and finishing the month's accounts. 'What did you know? And what's that daft hat you're wearing?'

Vic took it off and hung it from a coat stand. 'Keeps the dust off my hair.'

'You haven't got any hair! Want a cup of tea?'

'Okay, off my head then, and yes please.'

'So, what did you bleeding tell me, then?' Annabelle asked again as she got up to put the kettle on.

'We've got a darkie as prime minister, a Hindu, no less. Can't fucking believe it!'

'He seems a bit of a smoothie, I think.' Annabelle popped a teabag into each cup, and added three sugars to Vic's. 'I mean, he doesn't really *sound* like an Indian, and he's very rich, so maybe he knows what he's doing.'

'Oh, come on, Bella, don't talk rubbish. He's the one who spent billions during Covid, and for what? We still haven't recovered from that. But what does he care? It's not *his* money, is it?'

'Aren't you being a little bit harsh? Maybe judge him in six months' time, or a year?'

After Boris Johnson had been forced to resign as a result of Partygate, the contest to replace him had come down to a run-off between Liz Truss and Rishi Sunak, with the final decision as ever resting with rank-and-file Conservative Party members. During their campaigning, Truss accused her opponent of raising taxes as chancellor of the exchequer, and promised an economic revolution with high growth and low taxes. Sitting Tory MPs clearly wanted Sunak as their leader, but the Conservative members thought otherwise and more than 57% of them voted for Truss, who duly took over the reins in Downing Street.

Within days she and her chancellor, Kwasi Kwarteng, not-so-affectionately referred to as Quasimodo, announced a radical mini-budget, central to which was her promise of tax cuts, which her opponents claimed were unfunded. The financial markets went into turmoil, sterling plummeted, mortgage rates went up and the cost of UK government borrowing rose. Kwarteng was sacked, to be replaced by the Sinophile Jeremy Hunt, who immediately reversed her economic plan, even reducing her proposed two-year energy price cap plan to just six months. With the hyenas prowling ever closer, Truss resigned after only forty-five days in power, the shortest ever serving prime minister, and Sunak was installed in her place. The Conservative Party members didn't get to vote this time.

A year later, interest and mortgage rates were even steeper, energy bills were through the roof, inflation was skyrocketing, and illegal immigration was higher than ever.

'I was right, then,' Vic told Annabelle. 'That snake charmer is a globalist plant, pure and simple. And now the Yanks are sending cluster bombs to the Ukraine. I mean, cluster bombs, for fuck's sake. What is the matter with everyone? I thought cluster bombs were illegal.'

'Yes, you were right,' Annabelle sighed. 'And the Americans, like the Russians, didn't sign the agreement to ban cluster bombs. But unlike the Russian ones, which constitute a war crime if used in the Ukraine, the American ones are good ones, apparently. Work that one out.'

Hugh had been thinking along the same lines when it came to

Sunak. As he and Maria leaned on a fence watching the sheep being sheared, and Dominic made mud pies, he adjusted his hat and stated, 'You know, I now think that the chaiwallah was chosen by the Uniparty, and Truss just got in the way. She got the blame for a deliberate act of economic terrorism by those behind the curtain. I mean, there's no way a handful of days in power and half a dozen press conferences could have led to the damage they said it did; it simply doesn't make sense.'

'The chaiwallah?' Maria pushed her hair back and tied it into a bun. It was a glorious autumn afternoon, and she turned her face up towards the sun.

'Sorry, a bit derogatory, but it makes me so angry. The globalists clearly wanted Sunak, and they got him, bugger democracy. Now that he and Hunt – another totally slimy type in my view – are in place, they are putting the hurt on and dismantling the country. Wouldn't surprise me if, if and when Starmer is given his turn, the WEF people make him out to be a saviour, and before you know it, we'll be rejoining the EU. Though we still haven't really left. It's as if we don't even have the illusion of democracy any more; votes simply don't matter.'

Maria turned to look at him. 'That's a bit extreme. Have you been talking to Miles lately, by any chance?'

'What if I have?'

'Only I was talking to Delen the other day, and she said he was spouting the same views. I dread to think what Vic is thinking.'

'Well, we did have a chat, and yes, I guess we are thinking along the same lines. I suspect a lot of people are, but then the Brits are pretty apathetic these days. Come on, let's get Dominic cleaned up; he needs a bath before dinner.'

*

At that moment, Vic was in fact reading a poem by Rudyard Kipling which Annabelle had printed off and given him.

It was not part of their blood,
It came to them very late
With long arrears to make good
When the English began to hate.

They were not easily moved,
They were icy-willing to wait
Till every count should be proved,
Ere the English began to hate.

Their voices were even and low,
Their eyes were level and straight.
There was neither sign nor show,
When the English began to hate.

It was not preached to the crowd,
It was not taught by the State.
No man spoke It aloud,
When the English began to hate.

It was not suddenly bred,
It will not swiftly abate,
Through the chill years ahead,
When Time shall count from the date
That the English began to hate.

'Blimey,' Vic said as he looked up. 'I don't normally like poetry, but that's some poem! But do you really think that the English are *still* like that? Seems to me they prefer sitting on the sofa with their flat-screen tellies, ordering takeaways and living off bennies.'

'You might be right,' Annabelle said. 'But time will tell, won't it?'

CHAPTER THIRTY-SEVEN

Two Very Different Plans

Hugh polished off his two poached eggs, and then buttered some more toast before applying marmalade. 'I've got it,' he said to Maria, who was sitting across the table doing the *Daily Telegraph* crossword. 'After World War Two, which became the most successful economy in the world with no natural resources, *except their people?*'

'Enlighten me, then.' Maria put down her pen and buttered some toast for herself and Dominic. She poured herself another cup of tea, aware that this could be a long conversation.

'It was Hong Kong. And you know how they did it? Almost no government interference at all. They made people become self-reliant, none of this "managed decline", which has been our main political strategy since 1945. Maggie excepted, of course.'

'I thought you'd left politics behind. I need to get Dominic to school, and you've got some work to do, remember?'

'Yes, yes, I know,' Hugh said tetchily. 'I won't be long, promise, and it's just some thoughts I've been having. I mean, we're bankrupt as a country and national self-confidence hasn't been this low since the 1970s. None of our politicians could run a whelk store. We need something radical.'

'Okay, let's hear it, then. But quick, mind.' She glanced at her watch.

'Right, first off, national tax should be limited to 10% of GDP.' Hugh was counting his points on his fingers. 'Second, foreign policy should revert to the Castlereagh/Palmerston doctrine that there should be no naval or military interference anywhere in the world unless Britain is directly threatened. Next, it's clear that state education has failed, as has the NHS, so there need to be major reforms there; in fact, health should be people's own responsibility. And the police need to be depoliticised.'

'Are we nearly there?' Maria rose from her chair and began clearing the dishes away. 'I really need to get going. Dominic, go and put your shoes and coat on.'

'One minute! We cut the civil service by 80% and stop inflation-proofing public sector pensions; that's just immoral. We cap income tax at 15%, we turn back all the boats with the illegal immigrants, we stop indiscriminate welfare and get rid of all these regional parliaments, make the royal family self-sufficient, and ban the government from sending money abroad without a proper audit – you know last year we sent 17 *billion* pounds to the Ukraine, almost all of it totally unaudited. I'm sure there's something else I've forgotten.'

'I think that'll do for now; it's still only breakfast time. Come on, Dom, let's go,' and she headed towards the door, pulling on her own coat.

Hugh followed them to the car. 'But do you realise all of this would give the average family a tax reduction of 90%? You wouldn't need money from the state; people could afford almost anything they need out of their own income!'

Maria strapped Dominic into his seatbelt in the back of the Range Rover and gave Hugh a kiss on the cheek. She climbed into the front, started the engine and opened the window. 'It sounds marvellous, darling. I've no idea what you've been reading, but I suspect it's never going to happen anyway. But maybe send it to the Reform Party? They're looking for ideas. Anyway, I'll see you out in the fields in about forty-five minutes, maybe an hour.' With that, she turned the car and disappeared down the driveway, leaving Hugh in a cloud of dust.

'Shit,' he muttered. He was still wearing his slippers and had stepped into a puddle.

*

While Hugh was setting the world to rights, Vic was finishing the restoration of the basement in Westminster. All the rubbish had been cleared out, and leaking pipes replaced, while the miles of electrical wiring had been pulled together, replaced where necessary, and then secured with gaffer tape and installed in special guttering. The walls had been painted, and where there was evidence of asbestos, he'd installed plastic sheeting on the walls as a temporary measure.

Early on, while working alone, he'd created a deep hole in the flooring in which he now had several gallons of petrol stored, then resealed it with wooden planks and a thin veneer of concrete. It was in a corner and unnoticeable, and he'd covered the area with a cupboard where he kept various tools.

Now he watched as one of his employees, a big man from the southern Yoruba region of Nigeria called Kunle, tidied away the last bits and pieces and began to sweep the floor. He'd hired Kunle and a cousin of his called Tunde against his better judgement some six months ago – somehow or other they'd obtained British citizenship by pretending to be a gay couple escaping from Nigeria's draconian anti-homosexual laws – but they'd proved willing and able workers and Vic was happy to have been proved wrong.

Together with his two Sikhs, a couple of Poles and Ukrainians and his core of indigenous Brits, he'd created quite a diverse workforce. He'd drawn the line at Pakistanis, not least because the Sikhs had objected. Anyway, it was something the nobs from the Restoration and Renewal Authority had seemed quite pleased about, as if they'd ticked a box.

'Good job, Kunle, mate,' he said. 'Looking pretty spick and span. From here on in the maintenance should be more or less routine.'

'You bet, boss. You think them upstairs will be happy?' He pulled a red cloth from a pocket of his dungarees and wiped sweat from his forehead.

'I'm sure of it. Come on, let's finish up and get the others. I'll buy you all a beer.'

There were just four of them still working: Bogdan, a big Polish man with long blond hair tied back in a ponytail, Vladimir the Ukrainian, a small man with high cheekbones and a shaven head, who could have been a Tartar, and Kunle and Tunde. They retired to the Red Lion in Parliament Square, a Grade II listed Victorian pub and the closest to parliament, so a favourite watering hole of politicians, lobbyists and journalists. The beer was expensive, but it was a Fuller's pub and Vic liked their beer.

'Just a swift one,' Vic said. 'We'll drink outside, so that those who want to smoke can, and we don't have to sit next to all the plonkers inside.'

Bogdan immediately lit up, while Kunle went with Vic to help carry the beers.

'Okay, cheers!' Vic raised his glass to look at the amber liquid inside; the other three were drinking lager. 'That's camel's piss, that is, but anyway, good job well done, everyone.'

They clinked glasses and drank deeply.

'So, tell me, Bogdan,' Vic said, 'what do we call you for short: Bog?' Kunle and Tunde grinned. 'What are you spear-chuckers laughing at?' And they chuckled some more, because there was no malice in it.

'Actually, in Polish, Bogdan means "God-given", so you can call me God if you like.'

*

'You know, I've ended up with quite the multicultural workforce, and they're all good guys; who would have thought? I'm like the bleeding United Nations,' Vic said as he and Annabelle lay in bed that night. She was reading a book as usual, while he had his arms behind his head and was staring at the ceiling.

'It was never about race,' she said, turning her head. 'It's about integration, who wants to be here and adopt our way of life and contribute something. And there's some who will never integrate, even if they live here for a thousand years. They don't even want to, in fact; they'd prefer to turn us into a caliphate. But in the end, I don't really blame the migrants; they're just people looking for a better life. The really guilty ones are the politicians, and the media, and the judiciary. The Anglican church doesn't help much either.'

'Hmm. I suppose so.' He leaned over and switched off the light on his side. 'Well, enough of those happy thoughts; dream time. Sleep well.'

CHAPTER THIRTY-EIGHT

A Family Reunion

Miles and Delen were at home, taking tea in the kitchen, waiting for Piran and Wenna to return from their respective universities for the summer break. Neither had gone far; Piran had chosen Exeter, where he was studying Russian, while Wenna was in her first year at Bristol, studying computer science. It was raining and Miles had closed down the sea sports centre early.

'So, this CBDC malarky,' Miles said out of nowhere. 'It all sounds a bit sinister to me.'

'CBDC?' Delen picked up a biscuit and dunked it in her tea.

'Central bank digital currency. They've been talking about it for years, but now it looks like it's really going to happen. They want to get rid of cash.'

'They can't do that. What about car boot sales, local markets, church collections, things like that?'

'Oh, there'll still be some cash around, the change will be done gradually, but anything you have in a bank account will be controllable.' Miles pushed back his chair and finished his tea in a single gulp. 'I mean, I saw a clip of some guy speaking at the World Economic Forum saying that central digital bank currencies could be programmed.'

'Programmed how? What do you mean?' Delen had forgotten to take her biscuit out in time, and it had dissolved and dropped into her cup. 'Oh, damn!'

'He said that digital money units could be programmed to have expiry dates, or programmed so you can buy some things but not others. I mean, he tried to say that was a good thing, because you could be prevented from buying drugs or pornography, but you can see where this is headed, can't you? It's the thin edge of the wedge. Fifteen-minute cities and controlled money which you can only spend in approved shops and so on.'

'Crikey, are you serious? That sounds like total authoritarianism. When's it happening?' Now Delen was fishing around in the remains of her tea with a spoon to try to salvage bits of her biscuit.

'Maybe later this year, or next year; I don't know, but I don't like the sound of it.'

'Maybe we should buy some gold. And a fishing rod.'

Miles' mobile rang and he answered. 'Okay, on our way, be there in ten,' he said. 'They're both at St Erth station; let's go and pick them up.'

They put on their coats and dashed out to the car, a nearly new Honda HRV hybrid which they couldn't really afford but had seemed a good idea at the time. The rain was heavier now, and the windscreen wipers worked overtime during the short drive to the station, passing on the way a dogged demonstration outside the local school which Piran and Wenna had attended. Placards were held up with slogans such as *Stop the Perverts*, and *Leave Our Children Alone*, and *There Are Only Two Sexes*.

'What's that all about?' Miles asked.

Delen shook her head. 'Seems they've had some of those Story Time drag queens in to teach the kids about "diversity",' she said. 'I was talking to one of the mothers, you know, Bridie who works at Tesco? Her kids are at the school, and all the parents are up in arms.'

'Quite right too,' Miles said. 'It seems to be bloody Pride Month every month these days, and it *is* a perversion. I mean, I don't care what they get up to in their own homes, but now they're *so* in your face. Pisses me off.'

'Agreed. It's as if being white working class and a normal heterosexual is to be a despised and persecuted minority nowadays. The country has lost its moral compass.'

They found Piran and Wenna staring at their mobile phones in the station waiting room. Piran was taller than Miles now, but with the same unruly black hair, while Wenna took after her mother and was small and slight, with a smart and sensible bob cut. After greeting hugs, they loaded the luggage and drove off.

'We're going to pick up Grandma on the way,' Miles said, 'then Mum is going to cook us a nice roast leg of lamb for dinner, aren't you, dear?'

Molly was 105 years old now, but still fiercely independent and fully mobile, even if her sight was failing fast. As ever, she was overjoyed to see them all. Delen helped her into the front passenger seat and climbed into the back with her children.

'Terrible weather,' Molly said. Her hair was completely white, and she was wrapped up in a pink cardigan and wore thick stockings to keep out the chill. 'And I've got a leak upstairs, in the hallway; must be a loose tile. It's not much and I've put a bucket beneath it.'

'I'll have a look tomorrow, Mum,' Miles told her. 'Don't worry about it.'

The demonstrators were still standing outside the school with their placards as they got back to Carbis Bay.

'What's happening?' Molly asked as she twisted in her seat to look at the bedraggled group.

'Perverts are trying to teach the kids about trans rights, and how it's okay to be gay, and that there are dozens of different sexes. Some of them are only five years old, for God's sake. The parents don't like it,' Miles offered.

'There were only men and women in my day,' Molly observed. 'Even if some of them were queer, they just kept quiet about it. Nobody bothered.'

'Everyone's a nonce these days, Grandma,' Piran said from the back. 'Well, not everyone. I mean, I'm not, and nor is Wenna, are you, sis?'

She didn't bother to grace his comment with an acknowledgment, let alone an answer, but just kept looking at the rain out of the window. 'It's nice to be home,' she said.

Once inside the house and out of their coats, Miles poured them all a glass of wine, except for Molly, who took sherry. 'To us!' Miles toasted, and they all repeated his words. Delen excused herself and went to the kitchen to put the lamb in the oven, while Miles got the wood burner going and they all sat.

'These trans people and the BLM lot seem to have taken over the university in Bristol,' Wenna said. 'It's like they want to cancel everything and rewrite history. It's not right; history is history whether it's right or wrong, and the lecturers are running scared of offending anyone.'

'Even group chats and social media shut you down if they don't agree with your views,' Piran put in. 'I mean, what's the point of debating things only with people who agree with you? It's like an echo chamber. Political correctness is the same as communism in my view. Propaganda isn't about persuading or informing people; it's about humiliating them. You know, when people are forced to stay silent when they are being fed what are clearly lies, and even have to repeat them, they lose all sense of honesty and decency.'

'Some American presbyterian minister, a bloke called Chris Hedges, said that we now live in a world where doctors destroy health, lawyers destroy justice, universities destroy knowledge, governments destroy freedom, the media destroys information, religion destroys morals and our banks destroy the economy,' Miles said. 'A bit pessimistic, but then he's not far off either.'

'Well, on that happy note, shall we change the subject?' Piran suggested. 'Can we go surfing tomorrow?'

'If the rain eases, I'll take you around to Gwithian; surf's usually good there. And we need to fix Grandma's roof on the way.'

'What does it matter if it's raining? We're going to get wet anyway. As long as the surf is up, then I'm game.'

CHAPTER THIRTY-NINE

ASSASSINATION AND DISORDER

'Who is going to win, do you think?' Maria asked as she and Hugh helped a couple of farmhands pile haystacks into a barn.

'Win what?'

'The general election, of course; what do you think?'

Rishi Sunak had called for the election to be held at the beginning of December 2024, nearly two months early.

'Oh,' Hugh said, standing up and arching his back to ease the pain. 'Well, I guess the Tories will get hammered, but by how much is anybody's guess. And whether Labour pick up all the disaffected voters is another question. I can't see them winning back all their Scottish seats, and in England we could see a lot of people voting for the Reform Party or the Lib Dems or even the Greens, just for the hell of it.'

'I guess the biggest issue is the economy, as usual. And then immigration.' Maria also took a rest, wiping her hands on her dungarees and adjusting her headscarf.

'That's what Bill Clinton said, isn't it: "It's the economy, stupid"?'

'He also said, "I never had sex with that woman."'

'Yes, well, I think that was about something else.'

'And why do you think Sunak has called the election early?' Maria asked.

'I guess he figures people are more optimistic in December, you know, just before Christmas, whereas January is all doom and gloom, and we've got enough of that already.'

'Figures. Shall I go and make some sandwiches and bring them out?'

'Excellent idea; we'll carry on here.'

The election was held and the Conservatives lost, but not as decisively as expected. The 'red wall' voters still didn't trust Labour and many switched their allegiance to fringe parties such as Reclaim, Reform, or the Heritage Party, who between them picked up half a dozen seats. The SNP held on to their majority in Scotland, but only just after their vote was split by the Alba Party. And there were a surprising number of independents elected who owed no allegiance to any party.

The Tory party split, and Sunak resigned and headed off to America to enjoy his wealth. The rump of the Conservative Party chose as their new leader an old Tory grassroots favourite, Penny Mordaunt, a staunch Brexiteer, the daughter of a paratrooper and named after the naval cruiser HMS *Penelope*. The disaffected grouping, calling themselves the 'New Conservatives', were led by Boris Johnson attempting a comeback in politics. British politics was splintering.

Labour held a slim majority, but relied on the Greens and Liberal Democrats in key votes and struggled to implement any of their major manifesto pledges, which mostly seemed to rely on printing off ever-increasing amounts of money to prop up the ailing public services. The taxpayer was also expected to foot the bill for their 'net zero' environmental policies, which weren't working, while mass immigration continued unchecked. The pound slumped again and interest rates climbed steadily. The country was plunged into gloom.

'At least that Penny Mordaunt has big norks,' Vic said as he watched the evening news.

'Ever the intellectual,' Annabelle responded. 'What we have here is a perfect storm brewing. Next step should be a bit of lynching with a bit of luck.'

'Nah, the Brits haven't got it in them. Not like the Frenchies.'

'Sadly, I think you're right.' Annabelle swung her legs off the sofa and went to look out at the garden. It had started snowing, and a thin carpet of the white stuff covered the lawn. 'That's beautiful, I love the snow.'

'It's bloody cold, is what it is.' Vic went to stand with her. 'But yes, I guess it is kind of pretty. Shouldn't Alice be here by now?'

Their daughter was working as a lawyer in the city, but was coming home for Christmas, which was two days away.

'Probably the train is delayed. Wrong kind of snow, no doubt.'

Outside a car horn sounded, then the doorbell. Vic opened it to find Alice shivering on the doorstep in a faux fur hat and woollen coat.

'Dad!' She threw her arms around him and hugged tightly before releasing him. 'Can you lend me twenty quid? The cabbie wants cash, won't take my card. You'll get a fiver in change.'

'Hell's bells, how many times have I told you cash is king? Here.' He handed her a twenty-pound note and went with her to help with the suitcase.

*

Vic and Annabelle were both wrong when they assumed the Brits would never stir from their sofas, but it took a couple more years. Tony Blair was sitting with his wife Cherie and their three grown-up children in one of their favourite restaurants in Shoreditch, the police close protection officers at an adjacent table, when the waiter who had been serving them during the evening quietly approached the table and plunged an ice pick through the top of Blair's skull. His face was fixed in a rictus grin as he died, while Cherie's letterbox mouth opened in a silent scream. Two explosions rent the air as the close protection officers sprang into action, shooting dead the assailant, who later turned out to be a disaffected Serb whose family had arrived in the UK as refugees from Kosovo.

The assassination and the subsequent massive security clampdown served as the sparks to ignite sporadic riots which erupted in major cities across the country, fuelled also by recent electricity blackouts and huge disruptions in food supply chains because of ongoing civil disorder in continental Europe.

'Only nine meals stand between man and anarchy, as the old saying goes, although I don't know who said it,' Vic commented.

'But that bastard Blair got what he deserved.'

'And maybe people have finally twigged that governments don't give a shit about people, their children or their welfare, or their safety. All they really care about is holding on to power and getting more of it.' Annabelle was ever the cynic.

The rioting became more organised. Cars were burned in their hundreds; barricades were erected between the streets of different ethnic groups; jihadis armed themselves with weapons caches hidden in mosques, while criminal gangs on the other side produced their own alarming arsenal of assault weapons. Shops were looted, banks set on fire, and several serving politicians barely escaped with their lives after their homes were attacked by mobs. Similar riots had already been happening across a disaffected Europe, in Belgium, France, Germany, the Netherlands, Italy, Spain and even Switzerland. The war in Ukraine was still raging, and Moscow took advantage of the chaos in the West to begin a new offensive in the east and south of the country, while China attacked Taiwan.

'World's gone to hell in a handcart,' Vic commented. 'World War Three can't be far away.'

'And whose fault is that?' Annabelle asked. 'The politicians, and the media who have utterly failed to hold them to account.'

After a long hot summer, it took the military to quell the violence in most countries, although even that was a close-run thing, as many units, ignored by governments of all parties for years, refused to take up arms against their compatriots. In the end, both sides were exhausted and retreated to lick their wounds, eyeing each other warily. Food convoys were granted safe passage into the different armed enclaves. An uneasy peace reigned.

'I hope Vic and Annabelle are okay,' Delen said over a meagre supper of tinned tuna, home-grown tomatoes, cheese and bread in their kitchen. Their children and Molly had all come to stay with them for safety. 'Thank God the madness didn't reach us here.'

'It got close enough. Truro saw its fair share of violence; even the cathedral was damaged,' Miles replied. 'But I spoke to Vic, and they're fine, although they could see the fires raging across the river. Hugh and Maria also escaped the worst – most of the countryside did – but they couldn't move their crops, and they've got a lot of sheep now since the abattoirs were closed.'

'At least they won't go hungry,' Piran said. 'Maybe they could send us a couple.'

That winter, Molly passed away peacefully in her sleep, and was buried next to her husband at St Uny Church in Lannanta.

CHAPTER FORTY

AN UNNECESSARY DEATH

Vic and Annabelle might have escaped the worst of the collective madness and lawlessness that had gripped the country, but their own personal tragedy was waiting in store for them.

Despite their ages – Vic was entering his eightieth year and Annabelle her seventy-seventh – they were both still fit and healthy, and Vic especially fizzed with his usual nervous energy. He still had the Portakabin in Vauxhall and still made regular visits to Westminster for routine maintenance; he was by then a well-known figure to the police guards and, being self-employed, he had no need to retire. The very thought of retirement filled him with dread. Most of the other work pulled in by the company was carried out by younger men under his supervision.

They were walking together along the pavement to take lunch in one of the cafés built under the railway arches next to the Thames Embankment, when without warning a youth on an e-scooter sped up soundlessly behind them and slammed into Annabelle. She was flung into the air and fell badly, hitting her head on the kerb.

'Bella! No! No!' Vic ran to her side, momentarily torn between helping her and going after the scooter rider, who had picked himself up and was making a run for it. Vic clocked his face, a white kid, pallid with greasy dark hair under a black cap worn backwards.

'I'll find you, you bastard,' Vic said to himself as he cradled Annabelle's bleeding head and fumbled for his mobile to call an ambulance. He held her hand; it felt cold, and she looked at him with glassy eyes.

'Vic, my darling, I don't think I'm going to make it, it's all going dark,' she whispered.

'Yes, you are! Don't leave me! It's going to be okay, I've got you!'

'Just remember, Westminster, do it for me, and I'll see you on the other side. It's been good…'

Her voice was fading as he heard the siren of an ambulance coming from St Thomas' Hospital in the distance. He looked up, then stared in disbelief at the road, which was blocked by a slow-moving line of climate protestors in orange vests.

'Help me, someone!' he yelled. 'Get those scum out of the way, I need an ambulance!'

Several passers-by rushed to his side and covered Annabelle with their coats; others stood by and filmed the scene on their mobile phones. A policeman came to them.

'Clear the way! Get those idiots out of the way – my wife, she's dying!' Vic pleaded, tears streaming down his face now.

'We're doing our best, sir,' the policeman told him. 'The trouble is that it's a legal protest and—'

'Fuck your legal protest! Get them out of the way!'

The policeman ran off and tried pulling the protestors apart, but they kept reforming, ignoring the ambulance behind them. It was a full twenty minutes before the paramedics reached Annabelle, and by then they were too late. She was pronounced dead at the scene.

Vic was inconsolable and ran at the protestors, punching and kicking in his fury. Several went down with bleeding noses, one with a suspected fractured jaw and another with a broken ankle before Vic was restrained by two other constables who'd arrived at the scene. They handcuffed him and pushed him into the back of a squad car.

'They murdered her, they murdered my wife!' Vic spat at the officers, struggling against his manacles in the back seat. 'I'm going to kill them!'

The police officers were remarkably calm in response. 'I'd feel the same way,' one of them said, 'but you're not helping yourself, sir. This is not the way. We'll try to persuade the people you injured not to press charges. Now, we'll take you to the station and call someone, a family member or friend, who can come and collect you.'

Vic's head slumped forwards in defeat, and he began sobbing.

Alice collected him from the police station in Kennington Road an hour later. Remarkably, the police had succeeded in persuading the injured protestors not to press charges, mostly by impressing on them that public sympathy would definitely be on the side of Vic, which would damage their movement, and that they could be charged with involuntary manslaughter. Alice was still dressed for work in a dark trouser suit, and she too cried as she held on to her father, thanked the police, then helped him into her BMW 4 Series convertible parked outside.

She decided to take him back to Caversham, and she left the roof down, with the heating full on. He didn't speak for the entire journey, but just stared listlessly ahead.

In the house, she fixed him a large brandy and sat next to him on the sofa, stroking his arm.

'I can't stay here. She's all around me, but she's not here any more.' He spoke for the first time.

'I'm staying with you, Dad. I'll take time off work. I'm not going anywhere.'

That night he slept with the help of tranquillisers, but it was a troubled sleep and he awoke the next morning feeling washed out. He'd lost the will to live, Annabelle had been his rock, and without her he had nothing to hold on to.

Her last words kept going around in his head: *Westminster, do it for me.*

'I will, my dear, that I promise you, and then we'll feast together in Valhalla, or wherever it is that we all go,' he muttered to himself.

He took to wearing his red glass eye until Alice told him to take it out. 'It gives me the creeps,' she said. 'It's just weird, and you can't wear it for the funeral with everyone coming.'

Alice took care of the funeral arrangements. A memorial service was held at the small church in Mapledurham; the attendance was small at Vic's behest, although Miles, Delen, Hugh and Maria had all come. None of them were young any more.

Later, after Annabelle had been cremated, Vic stipulated that when his time came, he wanted their ashes to be mixed together before being committed to the sea. Miles promised that he would perform that task himself if he was still alive. He'd take a boat far off the coast, to where only the dolphins and seals would be witnesses.

CHAPTER FORTY-ONE

Pain and Anger

Time is supposed to be the great healer, but Vic didn't heal.

Miles and Delen went back to Cornwall and their lives carried on. Slowly the pain of losing their friend lessened, although Annabelle was never forgotten. The same was true of Hugh and Maria in Lincolnshire; the farm kept them busy, but often when Hugh was taking a rest and looking out across the flat, windswept landscape, he would think of his old friends and a great sadness would take hold of him. *It's hardest for those left behind,* he thought.

In time, Alice returned to work and Vic went to stay with her at their old flat in Chelsea, sleeping on the sofa bed in the lounge. He felt unable to be alone in the big house in Caversham, where they covered everything with dust sheets and set the alarm. But slowly his old anger returned. He knew he couldn't just give up; he had a promise to keep, and he also returned to work.

He decided to adopt a small dog from Battersea Dogs' Home, a mixed-breed mutt that he called Bowser: a funny little thing, nine years old already, which he fell in love with and which returned his affection tenfold.

When Vic went to Westminster, Bowser was happy to snooze in the Portakabin with the radio on; there was almost always someone on site, so he was rarely left alone. Otherwise, he sat next to Vic in the Jaguar as they visited various worksites, his head out of the front window, sniffing London's foul air, and they spent hours walking together in Battersea Park. In the evenings, Bowser was allowed to join Vic on the sofa as he watched television.

It was nearly a year before Vic returned to Caversham. There were things he needed to do which he couldn't do in the flat with

Alice coming and going.

'I'm fine now,' he told her before leaving. 'Come and see me sometimes at the weekends, or maybe I'll stay over here occasionally when I need to be at the office. Though going to the Portakabin is still hard; I don't think I'll ever be able to be there without feeling her presence.'

After endless hours on the dark web, researching how he could buy a delayed fuse for explosives, he came full circle and decided on the simplest of solutions. He knew he could never smuggle actual explosives into the House of Commons, and any kind of timer mechanism that had metal components would also be likely to be discovered.

In the end, he bought a hundred yards of thin hemp from a building supplier. In his garage he soaked it with potassium nitrate to oxidise it and create a long slow-burning fuse, not dissimilar to the ones once used in old warships to light their cannon. He reckoned it would give him at least thirty minutes, maybe forty. It had the advantage that it could be roughly handled, was virtually undetectable and, when lit, would burn slowly with a tiny glowing tip instead of flaring up. He also created a bundle of hundreds of matches, bound together with rubber bands, which he secured to one end of the hemp fuse. He was ready.

It was mid-afternoon when he walked to Westminster; the MPs should have finished their lavish lunches, and he expected the debating chamber to be packed. He had left Bowser at the Portakabin. The hemp fuse was wound about his body under a thick coat, and he passed through security without a hitch.

'All right, Vic? Bit of a chilly one today,' one of the guards greeted him as he passed through the metal detector.

'I'm sure it'll warm up,' Vic replied before walking on.

Down in the basement, he worked quickly. He pushed aside the cupboard and used a chisel to open a wide hole in the thin concrete covering, then slid out two of the wooden boards which hid the cans of petrol below. He hoped it hadn't degraded too much.

The lids were sealed and, lying on his stomach and reaching in, he gently prised one off, then the others. He then carefully lowered the end of the fuse with the bundle of matches, until it was an inch above the liquid, and secured the hemp around a leg of the cupboard. He used an unwound wire hanger to hook the rubber bands holding the matches, and ran the rest of the wire along the fuse, back to the cupboard leg, to prevent the matches falling prematurely into the petrol as the fuse burnt down.

He ran the rest of the fuse along the wall, back to the door. He listened, but heard nothing. He was alone, and he hoped no one would come down after he left, but then he wasn't coming back anyway.

He bent and held a lighter to the end of the fuse, and watched it glow. It slowly started to make its way back along the wall towards the cupboard.

Vic left the room and locked the door, then quickly made his way upstairs and outside, waving cheerfully to the guards as he exited from the building's front gate. He hailed a taxi to return to Vauxhall, less than a mile away, where he collected Bowser and his backpack, put on a black hoodie, and walked briskly back along the riverside to take up his position opposite Westminster.

CHAPTER FORTY-TWO

Retribution and Closure

He found an empty bench across the river from the palace of Westminster and sat down, putting his backpack by his side, while Bowser lay down at his feet. His one good eye was alert and full of anticipation. He shivered slightly, either from the cool early autumn weather or from excitement. He wondered if it would work; it was a primitive explosive, to say the least, but at least he'd tried. It was October 2034, and the sky was a mixture of sun and puffy white clouds, the latter scudding rapidly by high above while a brisk breeze ruffled the water's surface.

The timing was perfect; it was almost 200 years to the day since the palace of Westminster had been destroyed by fire, to be replaced by this gothic Elizabethan pile. He'd have preferred it to be exactly the right day for the anniversary, but this was close enough. It had been more important to wait for a day when the undersized and dysfunctional debating chamber was packed to the rafters, which was provided not by any debate about one of the great issues of the day, but by the members of parliament debating their own annual pay increase. That always got a full house. The House of Troughers, he called it.

He leaned forward in anticipation as a wisp of smoke trailed out of a lower window, then marvelled when a bright wall of flame suddenly burst into view with a huge *whoosh*, windows shattered and the smoke billowed. The flames took hold incredibly quickly, hungrily devouring ancient wooden panelling, floors and doors, fanned by the breeze. In the distance, the wail of emergency vehicles started up.

Vic chuckled and whispered a quiet 'Whoopi-de-do-da, burn,

piggies, burn' to himself. He knew Bella would have loved it, and been proud of him.

He dug into the backpack to pull out a packet of popcorn and a Thermos of tea, and sat back to enjoy the spectacle, which was quite the most beautiful sight he had ever seen. The dog jumped up next to him on the bench.

'Fancy some popcorn as well, do you, Bowser?' he said, scratching behind the dog's ears.

Together they watched as the fire engulfed the building, and Bower's ears twitched at the screams and shouts floating across the water. Fire and rescue boats arrived to join their colleagues on land, pouring foam and water onto the blaze, finally damping the worst of the fires, but too late to save the historic building.

Vic and Bowser watched for more than an hour. They had soon been surrounded by crowds of other people watching the spectacle, which gave them ample protection from the police searching for possible suspects; an old man and his dog attracted no attention. The chill of the evening air eventually started to make itself felt, despite the inferno across the river, and then they walked slowly back to Vauxhall.

'Fucking ace!' Vic said to Bowser. 'We did it!'

*

It was two days before the building was cool and safe enough for fire investigation teams to reach the basement, where they quickly discovered the source of the blaze, and Vic became suspect number one. One hundred and fifty-nine people had died in the blaze, a hundred and seventeen of them MPs. Vic counted it as a bonus when he heard on the radio that several in the press gallery had also succumbed. Dozens of others were injured, mostly with burns of varying degrees and smoke inhalation.

It was the same day that Superintendent Parker, retired, received a bulky letter at his home in Surrey. He opened it without thinking and a jumble of wires fell out, with a single sheet of paper.

As he read it, he became red in the face, his moustache twitching in anger. *You were close, Parker old boy, but not close enough. And now it's too late, we've finished the job.* It was signed *The Committee of Retribution.*

'No!' he yelled. 'Those bastards!' And he reached for the telephone to call his old office as his wife scurried into the room to see what the matter was.

The squad cars that pulled up outside Vic's house in Caversham were too late as well. The previous day, Alice had driven down, anxious that her father was not answering either his mobile or his house telephone. Once there, she rang the doorbell, but when there was no answer, she used her own key to open the door, and inside her worst fears were realised when she found Vic and Bowser curled together on the sofa in the lounge, both lifeless. They looked peaceful, as if they were dozing, and Vic had a small smile on his face. He had fed Bowser a strong dose of sleeping tablets mixed into his meal the evening before, and then taken the rest of the tablets himself with half a bottle of brandy.

Alice was numb with shock as she picked up the letter lying on the floor.

Darling Alice, she read. *Don't be sorry and don't be angry. This is what I wanted. I can't live without your mother and am going to join her, be happy for that. We were both immensely proud of you and will always love you. Remember what I asked about our ashes being mixed together and committed to the sea? Well, Bowser can join us in the urn as well. Forever yours, Dad.*

PS: When the police come, then yes, it was me. Your mother wanted it too. They had it coming.

PPS: We put the house in your name ten years ago, so they can't touch that. xxxxx

She was still in the house when the police arrived. She'd cried until there were no more tears left, and showed the officers the letter.

Weeks later, after Vic's body had been released and cremated, she drove to Cornwall to see Miles and Delen. Hugh and Maria were also there, as were Piran and Wenna. All had been in shock when they'd seen Vic's face on the television news and heard what he'd done, but somehow they weren't surprised either. They'd spoken at length to Alice by telephone; she'd poured her heart out to them and told them everything she knew.

'So that's what it was all about,' Hugh had whispered in disbelief. 'It was a long time in the planning.'

'Good grief!' was all Miles could say.

They boarded a trawler belonging to a friend of Miles and moved slowly out of the Heyl estuary at high tide until they'd passed the sandbank where Miles' father had died so many years ago. The powerful Merlin engines then took them two miles further out to sea, before they were cut and the boat rocked in the swell.

'They'll never be forgotten, that's for sure,' Maria remarked. 'They'll go down in history.'

'Well, whether they rebuild parliament or replace it with something else, let's at least hope it was all worthwhile and the powers that be have learned a lesson. Maybe we can pick up the pieces and start again and make a better job of it this time,' Delen added, an arm around Alice, who was crying softly, tears mixing with the salt air.

'People never learn,' Hugh said. 'We just go on making the same mistakes forever; that's the tragedy. But at least now we're back at the beginning of the cycle, so we might have a few good years before it goes sour again.'

Miles took the urn containing the ashes of Annabelle, Vic and Bowser and slowly poured them out over the water.

'Goodbye, old friend,' Miles said as they watched the brown smudge float away, then slowly sink below the surface. 'God bless.'

Acknowledgments: With special thanks to editor Harriet Evans, for her support and eagle eye, and invaluable input. Also, to close family and others (they know who they are) who cheerfully put up with the grumpy days.

Printed in Great Britain
by Amazon